# DEEP FREEZE

## VOYAGE TO NOWHERE

### D.S. WEISSMAN

**EPIC**
Press

# Voyage to Nowhere
## Deep Freeze: Book #1

Written by D.S. Weissman

Copyright © 2017 by Abdo Consulting Group, Inc.

Published by EPIC Press™
PO Box 398166
Minneapolis, MN 55439

Cover design by Dorothy Toth
Images for cover art obtained from iStockPhoto.com
Edited by Melanie Austin

LIBRARY OF CONGRESS CATALOGING-IN-PUBLICATION DATA

Names: Weissman, D.S., author.
Title: Voyage to nowhere / by D.S. Weissman.
Description: Minneapolis, MN : EPIC Press, [2017] | Series: Deep freeze ; book #1
Summary: When the world started to freeze over, the kids at the Samuel S. Fornland
    Boardinghouse had nowhere to go and no one to help them. James and his best friend Abe
    find hope in an abandoned cruise ship docked in the San Diego harbor. The only things
    standing in their way are the remaining kids from the boardinghouse and the scavengers that
    prowl the city.
Identifiers: LCCN 2015959221 | ISBN 9781680760156 (lib. bdg.) |
    ISBN 9781680762815 (ebook)
Subjects: LCSH: Adventure and adventurers—Fiction. | San Diego (Calif.)—Fiction. |
    Interpersonal relationships—Fiction. | Survival—Fiction. | Human behavior—Fiction. |
    Young adult fiction.
Classification: DDC [Fic]—dc23
LC record available at http://lccn.loc.gov/2015959221

EPICPRESS.COM

*For my family, you know why.*
*If you don't, you're out of the family.*

# THE DISAPPEARED

## JAMES

JAMES PRETENDED TO WATCH THE TELEVISION BUT THE CARTOONS didn't hold his interest as much as the hushed words of his parents in the other room. He lay down and pressed his head into a pillow to try and ignore the quiet argument emanating from the kitchen. If he raised the volume of the cartoon, his dad would scream, "Lower that goddamned thing!"

James had watched the same cartoon every day for the past month. A boy held a number of small balls and threw them to the ground. Animals popped out. The animals had powers. The boy didn't. The boy used the animals to battle, like a weird, popular dogfight. The boy wasn't good at it either. If James had been an animal with special powers he would have used them against that boy. James would have used his powers to protect himself from the outside world. He would have used his powers to envelop his body like the couch enveloped him now, creating a safe place to rest while the world in the other room quietly fell apart again.

"You keep saying it'll get better," James's mother said. "It hasn't."

Her steps were rushed and hard as she walked out of the kitchen and down the hall. She slammed the bedroom door shut. The crash shook the entire apartment. James's father slammed his fist into the refrigerator. James pressed the side of his face deeper into the pillow. His father stormed down the hall after her. He pounded on the door.

"Helen!" he yelled. "Stop it." The door rattled.

When James came home from school his parents often stood in the kitchen and turned away, engaged in a conversation they now had to keep quiet. His mom would wave but not smile. "Go watch some TV," she would say. His father would barely acknowledge him. James would turn on the TV and immediately hear, "Goddamn it, James. This is important." James would turn down the sound his father had turned all the way up the night before. His parents' conversation would continue and James would watch the boy throw the balls to the ground and wait for the animals to appear.

His parents' whispers became the intense soundtrack to the television show. James's father's breath heaved with impatience. James's mother grew irritated. The show continued with inching adrenaline until the final battle of the episode. The animals used their powers against one another. One animal would stand in victory, and the boy would raise his fist like he had fought the good fight. James's mother would storm off. His father would follow her, bang on the door, and eventually say, "We all know when it changed."

"Maybe we could take a cruise," his mother said.

"That's your solution to everything," his father said.

The first argument James remembered happened during *Sesame Street*. Oscar the Grouch whined about living in a trashcan and James's father echoed the same sentiment. James was young but he couldn't miss the lines in his life. The apartment was a square. The doors were rectangles. The refrigerator was two rectangles put together. The television was a rectangle. The toilet was an oblong. As he sat on the couch and watched the cartoon, the animals and the boy disappeared. Names crawled upward on the screen. The more James's parents fought, the more he imagined the world inside the cartoon: a life made of specific lines and colors and drawn by others. He imagined a story created and shaped by someone else and the power a person had over the lives in a story. James wished he had that kind of power now. The names continued to crawl on the screen and he watched the names transform into parallel lines. Every line that made every shape in the apartment became endless rows of parallel lines in front of him. He sat on the couch and watched them move and separate to create an unnatural grid.

The bedroom door clicked and opened. The lines continued to decorate the living room. The refrigerator didn't exist. The television didn't exist and neither did the names on the screen. The door clicked shut. His father had stopped yelling. The familiar sound of bedsprings followed the closed door. The thump of the bed against the walls followed the bedsprings. The lines blurred. The thump and squeak from his parents' room wrapped around the lines. Then James looked between the lines. He saw himself there filling the empty space at the center of the couch, exactly how he sat now.

The next episode of the cartoon started. The rock guitar filtered out the squeak and thump from the bedroom. James still didn't understand the cartoon. The opening credits made less sense. He turned it louder. The guitar drowned the familiar noise.

"I'm sick of this shit," his dad said. He came

out with a towel wrapped around his waist. He had more hair on his chest and shoulders than he did on his head. James's mom spent more time cleaning the apartment than his father spent grooming himself. "Keep it down or the television goes out the window."

"It's not that loud," James said. He kept his voice low.

"Stop mumbling," his father said.

"It's not that loud," James said again.

"Fine," his father said. "Then let's see if you can hear it from out there." He opened the window nearest the television, grabbed the set, and dropped it out the window. The crash rose up from the concrete drive. "Did you hear that?" His father walked away.

"What happened?" his mother said.

"We need a new TV," his father said and closed the door. James went to his room, crawled into his bed, and watched the ceiling. Shadows came and went with all the car lights that passed by. Each shadow formed an animal. Each animal had a power. James controlled them all. Instead of fighting against one another, they helped. They fought for other animals. They protected one another from wretchedness. Polar bears and wolves, dragons and snakes, deer and peacocks, it didn't matter. James brought them all together; they survived together. He drifted to sleep in the comfort of imagined battles and a newly formed animal alliance. When he woke up the house was silent. He couldn't remember a time when he slept through his parents' morning routine.

His mother made coffee. His father made toast and ate it in the shower. He would drop it, curse, and try to push the remainder of soggy toast down the drain. Sometimes when James took a bath his mother would have to dig out swollen pieces of soggy bread twisted with bits of back hair that hadn't made it down the pipe. James heard none of the ritualistic sounds of the morning. He walked out of his room. The kitchen was clean and unused. His parents' bedroom looked as if they had never slept there. The television was gone and left an outlined shade where it had been. The window had remained open. Remnants of broken glass and computer chips speckled the concrete. The marine layer made the windows sweat. James drew a happy face on the glass.

The apartment didn't turn into lines now. James sat on the couch and stared at the wall. He understood what it all meant. He had been the problem, the thing that changed. He saw it in the absence of the cartoons with wild and whispered emphasis. The sunlight came and went. When night washed over the apartment he wondered if the television would still work in fragments. He once saw a TV that could split into multiple screens. Some things can't be put back together, but others could still work after they broke. He looked back over the ledge. Any sign the television had lain there had disappeared. The happy face had disappeared.

James's stomach rumbled. He checked the fridge

and found an unopened box of baking powder and a putrid smell of rotting broccoli. He hadn't eaten anything since yesterday. His mother never stayed out past sundown and his father came home after work most days. No one walked through the door. He found the cupboards empty but freshly dusted. A box of crackers sat at the back of the highest shelf. He opened them too quickly and the top layers exploded from the packet. He held onto the box like a teddy bear. The crackers were salty and stale. He wanted to spit them out but hunger overruled him.

Footsteps echoed down the hall. He ran to the door with the box in his hand, opened the door, and looked outside. A large man with white hair and a silver mustache looked at him. He waved.

"Nice night," the man said.

James held onto to his cracker. He was shy around strangers and often hid behind his mother's leg at times like this. He stopped chewing on the cracker and tried to gain some courage. Neighbors knew each other. James had seen so on all the shows. That meant this man would know his parents.

"Do you know . . . " James said.

"Pardon me?" The man edged into his own door-frame across the hall. "I don't think I heard you."

"Do you know where my parents are?" he asked.

"I'm sorry, son," the man said. "Have you lost them?"

*No*, James thought. *They lost me.*

# A HOUSE, A HOME

## JAMES

THE SAMUEL S. FORNLAND BOARDING HOUSE WAS JUST A fancy name for an orphanage. James watched the television and wondered for a moment what his life would have been like if he hadn't come to this place. Everything had changed for him the morning he woke up and found the apartment empty. He hadn't always been alone, but people in San Diego hadn't always been confused about whether the flakes from the sky were snowfall or ash.

When James first stepped foot in front of the Samuel S. Fornland Boarding House, there was a hedgerow adorned with flowers and one tree that rose to the third story window. There was no snow and the weather would barely be cold enough for a dog with thick fur, let alone a polar bear. The door wasn't open; there was no one waiting for him with a smile, no one with arms crossed around their chests to protect them from the autumn wind. James remembered the rustle of leaves from the three-story tree. A few leaves spilled from the branches and glided down the block until they flew out of view.

James ran his fingers across the flowers. His soft fingers felt the likeness of silk, velvet, and wax, each petal different than the others. The colors were vibrant against Fornland's beige. The flower dipped inside itself like a cup he wanted to drink from. He wished the air were perfumed with flowers, with pizza, with the scent of something familiar on this unfamiliar street in front of an unfamiliar building, holding the hand of an unfamiliar person—not because he wanted to but because he thought he was supposed to. Her face looked as waxy as the petals felt; if the summer sun had stayed through autumn it would have melted the woman's face into a pool.

Her navy blue pantsuit would have been a pile of boredom on the sidewalk.

The woman knocked on the door, rang the bell, and finally entered Fornland, her hand light around James's hand. Her skin hesitated to touch his, as if whatever had happened to him was contagious, as if she feared the isolation and loneliness would spread until she were left alone and uncomfortable.

The entryway of Fornland was wide open. White tile squares spread across the room to the walls and the stairs in the distant corner. It was the largest and most confusing room he had seen, where the tile smelled of disinfectant, stairs were wrapped in steel and concrete, and the second floor started with a catwalk that disappeared around a corner.

They walked to the closed door on their right. James counted the tiles. When the woman knocked, she squeezed his hand a little tighter.

"It's open," a voice said.

But the door was closed and locked.

"It seems to be stuck," the woman said. She

twisted the doorknob once more but it ticked to each side. A click came from the opposite end of the door. A woman with dark skin, a confused smile, and dark eyes opened the door. Dark brown eyes that sparkled with gold gave ardor to her drained smile and husky voice.

The woman's grip lightened. "Bernice," she said.

"Pamela," Bernice said. "I thought you were coming on Saturday."

"It is Saturday," the woman said.

"Well shit," Bernice said. It came as a secret whispered into the door. She covered her mouth for a moment. James had heard the word before. His parents said it often enough, as did the TV they had watched, the movies, the music. "I mean—well it's too late now. Come in."

"Could we do the paperwork another day?" the woman asked. "I have someplace to be in about an hour. Monday maybe? You'll be here, won't you?"

"Honey," Bernice said. "I'm always here." She looked down at James, his hand still dangled in the fingers of the woman in the navy blue pantsuit. Bernice's voice softened when she looked into James's face. It was the first time in days someone had looked at him as opposed to past him or watched their own reactions in the reflections of his eyes, a play they had put on hundreds of times before; they recited the words and acted out the movements, but whatever emotion they needed had walked out on them—sometimes it was too hard to pretend. Bernice's voice made him feel comfortable, absent of labeling him a lost cause.

"You want to come in?" So many demands over the past days—the *where to sit*'s, *when to stand*'s, and *what to eat*'s—that a question tasted like candy when he repeated it in his head. He nodded.

"Guess I'll see you on Monday then," Bernice said. She closed the door behind the woman. Bernice's office was a large box filled with bookshelves and filing cabinets. Her desk was covered in papers stacked like cliffs against a rising tide.

"Want to know a secret?" James heard the jangle of keys and the clank of a lock unlatching. He continued to stare at her desk and the mountains and valleys of the paper world. The air ruffled. Slivers of light shined through the window. The waxy touch of flower petals gave way to the smooth handle of the wooden chair. James preferred the flowers. The lock latched. A Snickers bar landed in front of him. Some papers crunched beneath its weight and movement. She sat down in her chair. "I have an endless supply of these." She looked at James.

"It's true," she said. "For four years I have been able to reach into that cabinet back there," she pointed to the cabinet behind James, "and pull out at least one, if not two of these a day. My waistline hasn't appreciated it." The frumpy sweater and loose jeans Bernice wore were in line more with her office than her body, posture, and personality. "Little bit of a hell, really. Not that you have to worry about that."

She said the words with such nonchalance that it was obvious, even to a six-year-old, that she'd heard the words before from all types of kids. Even at six, James could see the lack of concern in Bernice's eyes about her language, and that her earlier concern was for Pamela's ears, not his. James would be hard-pressed to find a kid in Fornland that hadn't used that language before, let alone hadn't heard it.

"Take it," Bernice said. "It's yours." James reached for the Snickers. He tore the package open with his teeth but was careful not to bite into any of the chocolate. He saw two more bars on her desk, half-hidden beneath a leaning tower of paper. "What's your name, darling?" James didn't answer. His cheeks were puffed with chocolate and nuts like a starved squirrel. "Do you know what this place is?" James shook his head. "It's time to take the tour, I suppose. Any questions?"

"Where are my parents?"

The question brought Bernice pause. James had been silent for long enough to make any sound surprise people. Her eyes sank a bit. The question sat in front of him like a dead plant he kept watering, waiting for a sign of life. One green leaf and he could step away from the answer for good; only no one had the answer. He could tell by Bernice's face that she knew as much about his parents' whereabouts as he did. He decided in that moment that he would no longer care.

The phone rang, a high-pitched shrill muffled by the papers splayed around the room.

"I should answer that," Bernice said as she picked up the phone. The cord pulled and twisted around the paper stacks.

"Hello?" she said and cupped her hand over her mouth. She turned around to face the wall; her voice became a murmur. James watched her body lift and fall with her voice, but he didn't hear her words. He lifted his small hands toward the leaning paper tower, grabbed the two stray Snickers, hoping the wrappers wouldn't crinkle too loudly, and shoved the candy into his pockets. Bernice turned around and hung up the phone. James held his breath, worried he had been caught, wondering how he would be punished. What would his parents do if they were around? Then he remembered: he didn't care. As so often happened, the things he chose not to care about were the things he cared about most.

"I could give you plenty of answers," Bernice said. "But the truth is I don't know."

Hearing the truth from an adult felt new to James. He had spent his entire life hearing words but never meaning. He didn't want words; he wanted answers, but maybe, sometimes, it was okay not to know. He sunk his teeth into the candy bar.

"Let's go on that tour," she said.

Bernice showed James around Fornland. "It was a firehouse once. That's why it's so tall. That's also why there's a pole there. I don't know why we never took it out. Whatever." She showed him the dining hall, one of the living rooms filled with couches, and a television she said was the "bane of her existence."

"This is the Blend," she pointed to the room. "It's meant for the kids around your age until they reach about twelve. They're always fighting over the stupid television. I should take it out. Don't worry. I won't. Wouldn't have any leverage if I did."

James savored his Snickers. His other hand rested in his pocket, fingers rubbing the wrappers of the two stolen candy bars. He wanted to make them last. Bernice showed James the bathrooms, then the mixed study where a decent amount of books lined the walls and stayed "untouched." According to Bernice, it was a room where older and younger kids could hang out together, but was rarely used by anyone. She showed him the girls' side of the building and told him it was off limits to boys. Finally she brought him to the boys' bunks in a large room that was filled with beds. A hallway stretched along the far side of the room.

"This is where you'll stay," she said. "That hallway is where the older boys are. Your bunk is this one." She placed her hand on the bed frame. James's small bag was already on the bed. The room was empty of people. An awkward gray light came through the windows and shined the color of rotten lemons on the floor.

"Call it what you want. The boys call it the

Corral. The girls' side is the Collective." Her words whipped around the room but she didn't yell. "Maybe the boys feel like horses or wish they were stallions. You'd think it'd be the other way around: girls the Corral, boys the Collective. I never liked horses. I always thought of this place more as a dome, because of the echo. It's not so bad."

James stood next to what would be his bed. The bag looked as familiar as the room. It wasn't even his bag. A man had brought it to pack James's "necessities." Pants, socks, shirts, underwear, toothbrush, an extra pair of shoes, but they hadn't packed any stuffed animals or family photos because James hadn't had any. He was as indifferent to that bag and the bed as he was to the room, to the building, his parents—and the world he now knew to be indifferent to him.

"Can you keep another secret?" she asked. She bent down to look deep into James's face. Her breath had the aroma of the flowers he wanted to smell. "You look like you can." He nodded his head but didn't say a word. "Put out your hand." He did. "Should I trust you?" He took another bite of his Snickers, felt the thick wrappers in his pocket, and nodded his head again. He didn't blink. Blinking was a sign of mistrust. "I can take a chance, right?" She put a small key in his hand. She whispered in his ear. "Remember, it's a secret. Don't tell anyone or I'll want it back."

"The secret or the key?" he asked. His voice felt weak in his mouth. She smiled.

"Both," she said. "I think I can trust you. The boys should be back soon. It's Saturday, they always take advantage of a weekend. Make yourself at home." She walked out of the room. *The boys.* He wondered who those boys were, what their names were, what their lives were like before this place. But *before* didn't matter; James stuffed the key inside his pocket, unzipped his bag, and counted the remainder of his possessions, starting with the two stolen Snickers. At the time, they'd been a surprise treat, but later, after the Freeze started, they would come to represent much more.

He had no way to know what was coming. The Freeze would start in Europe. Rivers and lakes morphed into ice blocks, asphalt cracked from the cold. James and his friends hadn't paid attention because they weren't European. The Freeze crossed the ocean and made it to the East Coast. New England was pummeled with blizzards. Snow flooded the streets of Boston high enough to render snowplows useless. Some people exchanged their cars for snowmobiles. James hadn't cared because he didn't live on the East Coast. Then the snow began to blanket the Midwest and creep closer to California.

It had been nearly ten years since Bernice gave James those Snickers. James sat in the Blend with Abe and Elise. The news was on in the background. James hadn't been listening.

"When was the last time it snowed in San Diego?" Abe asked.

"I always wanted to see snow," Elise said. "And a polar bear."

"You have," Abe said.

"When would she have seen snow?" James asked. "Or polar bears?"

"On TV," Abe said.

"Probably," Elise said.

"Probably," Abe repeated.

"Smart ass," James said.

Abe and James had been best friends from the moment Abe had entered Samuel S. Fornland. Elise came a few years later. She and Abe had been together ever since. Abe's parents had died in "a collection of drug overdoses," Abe liked to say, rather than the singular overdose it took for death to occur. Abe thought of his parents as invincible, James knew, where no mere drug could have stricken them down, therefore it took collected abuses to stop their hearts. Elise's mom had dropped her off. James's parents had evaporated.

Their worlds had been tearing themselves apart for years, but for a brief moment they were excited to see the snow.

# CLOSING DOORS

## ABE

MOST OF THE KIDS THAT HAD CALLED FORNLAND HOME left when the fires started. These weren't the fires that swept through the dry brush of rich people's foothills. James and Abe dreamed of wild-fires as kids did, the heat pounding their faces, the orange blaze rising into the sky; they would be strapped in their firemen's gear, single-handedly extinguishing the flames, the firestorm replaced by the gentle hiss and sizzle of smoldering timber.

After the snow started, fires became born of despair, showing a hopelessness that spread through the spirit and the mind.

When the snow started, San Diego rejoiced.

Southern California had been in a continuous drought for several years. As so often happened, on the fourth day people's enthusiasm waned. On the sixth day people didn't want to go outside. People that lived on sunken and poorly guttered streets started to have trouble with their doors; the snow piled higher each day. The snow shovel became a sought-after commodity. People had thought they could endure, like the East Coast endured so often, like Russia, or parts of northern Asia had endured frozen winters. No one wanted to admit that once the snow began to fall, it was too late. By the fourth week, the city's sense of order started to crumble beneath the weight of those that had already given up. They felt the pressure of endless snow piling on top of them.

When the world started to change, Abe was young. Youth equaled powerlessness, and Abe became indifferent. Politics, hunger, snowfall, overdoses—it was all the same in the end because he couldn't do anything to stop or even fix it. Abe had watched his powerlessness turn into fear when the needle stuck out of his mother's veins. The tiny hole in her arm where the needle was wedged had trickled with droplets of brown blood that ran down the bend of her elbow, dripped onto the floor, and seeped into the stained carpet where the droplets blended in.

Abe was just as helpless when the paramedics smashed through the door, ran to his father, and tapped his face to open his eyes, which, at the time, rolled around like bloody ping-pong balls. Abe's father's pupils were gone, leaving only the blood-shot whites of his eyes. His father was on his way to death; it was obvious. Though Abe's mother lay dead with her arm draped across the tears in her jeans and sludge leaking from her body, it was the look on his father's face that he would associate with death. The bright red whites of his father's eyes brought with it the look of a stranger, someone Abe couldn't recognize. Drool formed a waterfall from his father's mouth and pooled around his dark beard until it plummeted onto his black shirt where the spit hid behind the darkness of the clothing.

Abe had tried to memorize every second of that moment: the color of his parents' clothes, their hair, the looks on their faces, how many veins he could count in their arms. His father wore shorts; his mother wore tight jeans. Had her hair been up? Had there been some gray in his father's beard? The more he thought about the day, the less he *knew,* and the more he questioned. He knew the paramedics slapped his father's face. He knew the look of death in his father's eyes. He knew the medics had wrapped his father onto a gurney and taken him, leaving his mother in a crumpled heap on the floor with the needle stuck in her arm. Abe stayed quiet and followed the gurney like a ghost, hopped onto the ambulance, and tried to hide his fear but not his body. He remembered the moan of the sirens. They hurt his ears even while inside the ambulance. The driver took the corners at a speed that made Abe's knuckles turn white when he gripped his seat. He tried not to slide across the bench.

The chairs in the waiting room were lined with scratchy fabric that rubbed against the back of his neck. The tile looked as stained as the carpet back home under the glaring yellow lights. He didn't think about where his mother was or where she would be or why she wasn't with him at that moment in the room; why she didn't drape her arm around Abe as they waited for his father to be released from the hospital . . . again.

A woman in a blue pantsuit entered the room. She had flat soles, no heels, and a waxy face. There wasn't much to remember about her when he wanted so much to remember the rest of the day. He wished he could rid himself of his father's eyes and the jagged needle that pointed out of his mother's arm as if there were a magnet in the air.

"Is your name Abe?" the woman asked.

"Yes," he said. He was never taught not to talk to strangers.

"My name is Pamela," she said. "It's nice to meet you." He nodded. Abe hated that he could remember the conversation with the woman he met once. He hated that he could remember her waxy face and pantsuit, that she took him away from the waiting room and into the open tile of the Fornland entryway, when it was clear his father would not be released and his mother would not be waiting with fresh macaroni and cheese, the blue box with the powder cheese coating each noodle. It tasted better than melted, muddy cheese. Pamela had said the words.

"I'm sorry Abe, but you're parents won't be coming back."

"Back from where? Where did they go?"

She shook her head and said a word he knew but couldn't understand. There was a list of words and emotions Abe realized were harder for adults to say and feel because they had felt them before. Death was one that hung thick on their lips, unable to fall away. Like pain, where Abe wouldn't cringe at the mention of a paper cut because he had never had a paper cut before, but Abe understood pain. Abe understood death. He just hadn't had to experience it in the way that, at the moment, almost crushed him, not because he didn't understand what the words meant, but because he couldn't understand how those words pertained to him.

When Abe entered Fornland, the tiles in the entryway had been whiter—less stained—than they were by the time the snow fell. He had crossed his arms and stuffed his hands beneath his seven-year-old lack of biceps. Pamela knocked once on the door and didn't wait for an answer. She opened the door and a woman with chocolate eyes sat behind a desk covered in candy wrappers and paper mountains.

"I didn't think you would be here until Wednesday," Bernice said.

"It is Wednesday," Pamela said. "This is Abe."

He kept his hands beneath his arms. His face stayed sour. He wanted to go home and sit with a steaming bowl of mac and cheese with cartoons loud on the television.

"Would you like to sit, Abe?"

Pamela took a seat and left the second chair open for Abe. They weren't like the seats at the hospital. The wooden armrests were smooth and cool. The cushions were slick and comfortable. The woman pushed papers toward Pamela. She pulled a pen from her pantsuit breast pocket. The scribble of pen on paper filled the room and covered the silence between Pamela and the woman, between Abe and Pamela, the woman and Abe. When Pamela finished her scribbles the click of the pen retracting was louder than the original, tenuous click.

"Good seeing you Bernice," Pamela said. "As always."

"Hopefully I'll see you later than sooner," Bernice said.

Pamela turned, a small smirk pulled at one corner of her lips as if the feeling were mutual. Abe didn't say much to Bernice. Bernice didn't say much to

Abe. His shirt pressed into his nose and he caught some scent of his father in his clothes. He wasn't ready to pull his shirt over his face and take the entire smell away at once. He wanted it to linger for as long as it drifted away, the final details of the last day they had together.

Bernice brought him into the large open space of the communal bunk. There was one boy left in the room. He made his bed. Most of the beds weren't made; the sheets spread across the mattresses in a collection of crashed waves.

"James," Bernice said. "This is Abe."

James nodded. Abe kept his arms folded.

"Make sure he knows what to do," she said. She put her hand on Abe's back. Her chocolate eyes looked at his arms. She looked into his seven-year-old eyes and he knew she wanted to say something, or she felt something, but he couldn't explain it any more than he could explain what pain and death meant to him.

"He'll take care of you." She walked out of the

room. James nodded to an open bed. Abe's bag was already on top of the mattress. Abe figured that's what Bernice meant, that James would show him around, or help him settle in, help him understand what had become of the world. James finished making his bed and threw a Snickers bar onto Abe's bag. Abe uncrossed his arms, picked up the Snickers.

"I don't like nuts," Abe said.

"Eat it anyway," James said before walking out of the room.

Abe ripped open the wrapper and took a bite. The chew, the crunch, the richness, somehow it made him feel a little better. He took another bite. He was alone in the room. Flecks of dirt floated through the beams of light that shined through the stretch of window sectioned off into small squares.

*So much for taking care of me*, Abe thought. He had spent enough time taking care of himself anyway. As the sun started to fade from the room and light from the dim yellow bulbs spread across the concrete floor, Abe couldn't stop thinking of the candy bar, of James, and the conviction in James's voice. *Just eat it anyway*, as if he knew that a piece of chocolate would make this place bearable. Somehow it had. James was young and should have had no impact on the world, *like me*, Abe thought. Youth equaled powerlessness, but James was young and, with a piece of chocolate, somehow James made the world feel different to Abe.

# UNFORGETTABLE FACES

## JAMES

S AN DIEGO WAS SPREAD ACROSS THE VALLEYS AND MOUNTAINS of Southern California, bordered on the east by a frozen desert, and a slowly freezing ocean on the west. Bernice had stayed for a while. James had always liked her. She was nicer than the families James had spent little time with, including his own. There were three hundred forty-six kids of all ages in Fornland, and Bernice was in charge of them all.

The boardinghouse had always been a product of sparseness. Bernice stood at the top of the pyramid, yet supported them all at the same time. James could remember a stout woman who watched over the kitchen and an effeminate man who watched over the laundry. Fornland was guided by adults but run by kids, a type of jail run by the unjustly incarcerated.

Bernice had a family of her own, two daughters and a son, of some age James didn't remember. He had watched her life change from a distance, from when he was six and she wasn't married, to now, when he was fifteen and her kids were old enough to be scared of this place. It made James laugh a little, that his life might be used as a comparison to the haves and have-nots of other people.

It wasn't long after the first building bash that Bernice had decided to leave Fornland. The building down the street exploded into a pile of rubble. Heaters, kerosene, and all types of heating equipment were stolen. The block had filled with people wanting to stand around the fire, the ones who weren't able to warm themselves during the increasingly cold nights. Maybe that was the real reason the city began to burn, to save people from the cold—but the embers stopped crackling and the fire disappeared.

"It was the warmest I'd been in months," Elise had said.

"You shouldn't have been there," Abe said. "I'll take care of the cold."

"What does that even mean?" Elise asked. "You'll make it go away? You have that kind of power?"

Abe and Elise had been together for so long it seemed like their ages jumped from sixteen to seventy-five; they were married to how things once were and yet always bickered about who they had become.

"Wouldn't you have gone, James?" Elise asked.

James wanted to stay out of the fight. It didn't matter whose side he took, he would be wrong. The city had become dangerous, not because of the cold, but because of the people. The colder it became, the wilder the city had become.

"It is getting dangerous," James said, looking at the floor.

Bernice sat in her office staring at the diminished stack of paper. Elise pulled James and Abe into the office for Bernice's opinion.

"Bernice," Elise said. "We need you to settle some—"

Bernice looked at the trio with a distant stare. Her tired smile had gone. The glitter in her eyes had disappeared.

"Your office looks nice," Abe said.

"Cleanest it's ever been," James chimed in.

"What's wrong with going to the building bashes?" Elise asked.

"I can't stay," Bernice said. James knew the day would come when she would choose her family over Fornland—the people who loved her and those whom she loved more than the kids she babysat. There was a part of him, the part that had seen her stay this long, that convinced himself all this cold would blow over.

"You can't go," Abe said. "This place won't last without you—we won't . . ."

Elise stayed quiet. She wrapped her hand around Abe's and stepped closer to him. Bernice stared at James.

"We need you," James said.

"You haven't needed me for years," Bernice said. "This is all the paper left in Fornland. Use it last, only when you need it most." She stood up and walked slowly to Abe and Elise. They hugged her tight. She walked to James. "Honest, you haven't needed me for years." She hugged James. His head once barely reached her chest; his arms couldn't wrap around her skinny body, but that was a long time ago. He was taller than her now, able to wrap her in his arms.

"Elise," Bernice said, "stay away from the fires. Those people are animals. It's only going to get worse." Just like all their parents before her, Bernice left.

Rumors began to spread and the kids began to trickle away. Some kids left to search for the parents they were convinced were out there. Others heard tales of Central and South America maintaining pockets of heat; some kids just didn't want to spend the remainder of their lives inside a beaten-down home for troubled children. Then there were those like Abe and James who remained committed to some sense of connection, to each other, to the house, to the fear of what the world would be like outside. San Diego had become a battleground filled with people fighting for a hell that was either frozen or burning to the ground. The real question James asked himself as he watched the house empty little by little: *Where would I even go?*

Four hundred and twenty-seven faces ran through his mind, each face another in Fornland; that's what his life was, and he knew his life in the boardinghouse was better than any other life he could have, should have, or would have lived by now. Maybe that is why he remembered the faces of all the kids who had come and gone—to not lose himself in the malaise of disappearing—where if he held onto their faces, whether he knew them or not, he could hold onto himself. He remembered less of his parents' faces; he resented their faces—his father's mustache and his mother's curly hair.

It had taken him two months to say anything to any of the kids in the boardinghouse. James stayed to himself most often. The first words he had said were at dinner when he asked the kid with the scar over his eyebrow to pass the salt. His name was Francis, he preferred to be called Karl, but everyone called him Yarn because no matter what shirt he wore, or how many times he tore the string from the fabric, there was always another string to unravel. Yarn was eight years old. He and James arrived around the same time in the Corral. Yarn almost hit the crier-mark; he had cried for seven out of ten days. On the seventh day he had some sort of epiphany and accepted that life outside the boardinghouse wasn't possible.

There was a moment when people started calling James "Salt." *It doesn't take much to earn a nickname in this place,* James had thought. The nickname didn't stick. After that first time he asked Yarn for the salt, James never asked for salt again.

There had been a putrid perfume in the air since James's parents had walked away. He tasted it every time he opened his mouth. He chose not to speak instead. He had sat at the table to eat dinner, sloppy joes. Even at six years old James knew there couldn't have been a more clichéd meal in an orphanage than sloppy joes. He shook half the salt onto his elegant mess of sloppy joe, so much that the chili mound on his plate looked like it had contracted lice. James took a bite and almost chucked the forkful in his mouth, along with the two Snickers he had eaten for lunch.

"You have to try harder," Bernice had said earlier that day in her office. "You've been here two months and you don't have any friends. Not that the staff has seen, not that I have seen. You can't go through life removed from everyone else." She left the room for a moment. When she came back, James's pockets were stuffed with king-sized Snickers. He started to think she had them there for him on purpose. He hadn't used his key to the Cage yet.

"I think you'll find this place to be not so bad," Bernice said.

"It isn't as bad as I thought," James said. He felt the crinkle of the candy bar wrapper in his palm. He wanted to get out of Bernice's room as fast as he could because he worried the candy would melt in his pockets before he had a chance to eat it.

James's candy bar lunch was the closest he came to luxury, and he held the flavor of chocolate and nuts in his mouth, refusing to let go of the one good thing he had found since before his parents left. At six years old, he knew that his life would be plagued by the absence of his parents, but he didn't realize it would start with the memorization of Yarn's face.

James spent the remainder of dinner with his fork shoved deep inside the salty mound of sloppy joe. He pushed the slop around his plate, turning the chili into molehills and mountains. He created valleys and canyons with the brown sludge, until the salt disappeared somewhere. He molded a new world on his plate. He had shaped a brand-new earth with his own hands. But he would throw the entire plate into the garbage before taking another bite.

Yarn took two pieces of flimsy white bread and smashed the slop over one piece. He slammed the second piece on top of the mound. The sloppy joe seeped out of the sides of the bread, back onto the plate. His elbows rested on the table. The scar on his eyebrow was bleached white like the bread. He took one bite and the inside of the sandwich slipped through the soggy crusts, splattering against the table. *Yarn's biggest mistake*, James thought, *was that he wore a white shirt on sloppy joe night*. Yarn had an endless supply of white shirts that he wore at the worst possible times: sloppy joe night, greasy sausage breakfasts, spaghetti night. Somehow, when he washed them, they always came out cleaner than when they went in—the speckled grease ousted from the pristine white glow, another piece of thread hanging from the sleeve or the hem.

In the years that followed, James always remembered the scar that made Yarn's brown eyes as sad as the grease sprawled across his shirt. Yarn's face was number one of four hundred twenty-seven, not because of the scar alone, but because he was the first to leave Fornland.

In Yarn's absence James saw his face all over the Corral. An image of Yarn's scar draped the sheets of his old bed. His sunken eyes held the despair of spaghetti sauce splattered on his white shirt, but it always ended up okay; the sauce washed away. James saw the shirts in the same way he saw Yarn, one large mess that came out clean on the other side of the wash. After James's first three months at Fornland, Yarn was picked out of the pile of messy children, rung out, cleaned up, and taken away by a new couple, all fresh and clean.

The moment someone left Fornland they would have what James wanted, a way out and something to look forward to, even after the snow fell. The ones who left had hope. He hadn't eaten any of the food from the kitchen those first two months. He had scrounged for scraps and vending-machine extras, until he gave in that night. The moment he put the food to his lips, he belonged to that place. The moment the grease of the sloppy joe dripped onto his lips, hope left him. He became another face in the Fornland crowd, except his face would never be a part of the four hundred twenty-seven.

# EMULATING HEROES

## JAMES

A FIRE POLE REMAINED AS PART OF THE COMMON ROOM, THE hole now filled in. When the firehouse moved sometime in the nineteen eighties, the walls were left to decompose and drift into obscurity, much like Samuel S. Fornland—the first fire chief of the station—who died saving a baby from a fire. Fornland crawled out with the baby in his arms, smoke in Fornland's lungs. The story said he passed the baby to the mother, the mother cried, the baby laughed, and good old Samuel fell to the floor with an exasperated gasp. The story was written on a plaque hanging in the entryway of the house. The plaque was never taken down. When the boardinghouse moved in, Bernice decided to keep the name Fornland because they were still saving children. That was the story passed down through the kids, by the kids, for the kids. It was rare to find anyone in the system that felt like they had been saved.

James couldn't imagine himself saving anyone. When he and Abe dreamed of fighting the constant threat of fires on the outskirts of the city, it was Abe who dove headfirst into the fantasy, surrounded by flames in search of a child, carrying the defenseless babe out of danger. James stayed on the border of the flames with a fire hose. Abe would crawl out of the fire, his best impression of Fornland, while James took down the flames one by one by one. The story of Fornland to anyone outside the boardinghouse was nothing more than forgotten history, because that's what the world did—gave you life, left you memories, and made sure to forget you.

The first story James ever heard from some source other than the television was from Bernice. She would read to the corral and the collective every

Friday night—most Friday nights. It was almost ten days after James had arrived in Fornland. It was weeks before his first bite of terrible food that he had salted for no other reason than to get the bad taste of life out of his mouth. Most of the corral moved their beds into a circle to try and get as close to Bernice as they could. It was a calculated movement, one that showed they had done this countless times before. The bed frames scraped against the tile and the light outside faded behind the buildings. The fluorescent lights of the Corral gave way to the flashlight in Bernice's hands. The book shined and became a candle between her fingers.

The name glowed gold against the night sky painted on the cover.

"*The Little Prince*," Bernice said. James heard whispers crawl from the shadows of the encircled space.

"This is my favorite," a bird-nosed boy said.

"I love this story," a boy with a bowl haircut said.

They were words James wanted to understand,

but he had never heard of that book. Up to that point he had never opened a book other than the Chinese food menus wrapped around the door handle of his old apartment.

Bernice said the author's name, read the beginning lines, and showed them all a picture of a boa constrictor wrapped around an animal, its mouth opened, and the animal's eyes wide with fear and a lack of oxygen.

Bernice read the story aloud, telling the tale of a boy who had drawn snakes that looked like hats. Adults didn't understand his masterpieces, the art the boy had drawn to scare and surprise the adults. They questioned the drawings, which made the boy question himself.

James's mind began to reel at the possibilities of boa constrictors, of the wonders of life that he failed to conjure. What worlds were outside of his mind where more than one kind of snake had the ability to wrap its entire body around another animal and swallow it whole?

When the boy's drawings were misunderstood he chose to be a pilot instead.

"He learned to explore the world differently," Bernice said. "The narrator learned to explore the world by flying across it." It was the first time James thought about the possibilities of exploring a world that wasn't San Diego, a world that he was a part of but also removed from. He sat with his knees to his chest, his elbows on his knees, his hands wrapped around his chin. If his mind was in fact made out of gears and metals, he could feel them turn.

The scarce light had slithered through the window leaving the flashlight in Bernice's hands the brightest thing in the room. No matter how many pages she turned, James couldn't get past what she had read earlier.

*They always need to have things explained.* Grown-ups always needed to have things explained. What happened to people between the ages of six and grown up that turned them soft-minded? How was it that children between the ages of five and twelve, stuffed inside a box, understood the world more than adults? James wanted to get all of the lost adults in a room and shove the first rule of life into their mouths: don't abandon your children.

In the throes of Saint-Exupéry, within the hands of *The Little Prince*, James found a sense of clarity in his six-year-old mind that most people couldn't find after cleaning their bedroom. The world was different than it should be; he was different than the world; the word *fair* was meant for nothing more than baseball and playgrounds. In ten years, when James would hold himself on the railing of a ship escaping the horrors of San Diego and the disgusting taste that lingered in his mouth for far too long, he would look upon the endless ice and think back to Bernice's voice. Her words were filled with a sense of awe that spread like fingers tickling up and down his back. Her words gave him ideas that he never knew he could have and might never know again. In that moment he would think he saw the Little Prince's face, one of four hundred twenty-seven faces he could never and would never forget. Bernice's words would breathe into his ear as the cold, still air turned his cheeks pink.

Bernice read the sentence about the landscape, describing it as both sad and beautiful, and James learned that some things in life could be both.

He listened to Bernice say those words plenty of times; she would hold up the book with the flashlight on the pages. The entire landscape of the desert glistened like a bank vault filled with golden dreams. James agreed with the book, with Bernice, that first time, the second time, the third, fourth, fifth, sixth, and seventh times. Over his years in the Corral he would look around the quiet chaos of the strewn-about beds, corrals sprawled out over the mattresses and floor with their eyes running to the light like moths because no matter how much of himself he lost when he first arrived at the boardinghouse, so much of Fornland too quickly became a part of him.

In Fornland he could press his fingers to a book page and see if the colors smelled like they looked.

It was lovely. It was sad. It was his. It was someplace he felt he deserved. No matter how much he hated Fornland—because he always would in the way that someone blamed mustard for making them vomit when in actuality they had the flu—James would stay connected to the books Bernice read, to the shouts and screams of unsupervised children in the night, the initial gag of the too-salty sloppy joe that dragged him down to the level he never expected to crawl out from.

Bernice had told him the first story he ever heard, read him the first book he ever felt like reading. It wouldn't be the last. And the stories of a better world would start to fall around him like maple syrup, full and sticky, to try and give the kids of Fornland the better lives they all wanted. James came to believe that what they deserved was each other.

# ABSENCE OF UNDERSTANDING

## ELISE

ELISE BELIEVED IT WAS HER FEAR OF BLOOD AND SHOTS THAT brought her to Fornland for quite some time after she arrived. She was the type of child that ran from shots. She couldn't behave and her mom was tired of it.

"Why can't you just do what you're told?" her mom had said. "It's just a shot."

Elise was one of the few who wasn't taken to Fornland by Pamela, the same woman who had brought Abe and James, even Charlotte. Elise's mom dropped her off, telling Elise she was going to meet her new babysitter. She did, in a way.

Elise once spent weeks at her grandmother's

house. Her mom dropped her off in the morning and came back three weeks later. Elise had gone to her grandma's with pink socks, jeans that were too big, a bright blue shirt, and a kitten backpack with one magazine where she could look for hidden images, a pack of colored pencils, and no paper. When her mom came back the colored pencils were worn down to their nub. Elise wore the same clothes. The jeans fit her by then. That was how it felt with Fornland, too.

Elise's mother took her out of the car.

"It's just for a little bit," she had said.

"How long is that?" Elise asked.

"You have everything you need in your backpack."

"How long will you be gone for?"

"I'll see you when I get back."

Her mother knocked on the door.

"I love you," she said and got in the car. She never waited for the door to open.

"Who are you?" Bernice said.

"Mom said you are my babysitter," Elise said.

"Where is your—who are you?"

"I'm Elise."

Bernice brought Elise into her office, sat her down in the same chair Abe had sat in, the same chair James had sat in. It could have just been a coincidence but when Elise, Abe, and James shared their Bernice stories, they remembered sitting in that same chair, as if that chair brought them together. James said he wanted to know if everyone always sat in that chair or if, for whatever reason, those who sat in that chair grew closer together than the rest.

"What's in your bag?" Bernice had asked.

"Everything I need," Elise said.

"Is that so?" Bernice asked. "May I look?" Elise handed Bernice the bag. Bernice looked. "All you need are colored pencils, an I-Spy magazine, and a pack of Starburst?"

"Starburst are my favorite," Elise said.

"Where are your parents?"

"My mom will come back."

Elise didn't say it with a sense of certainty but with a sense of hope. She wasn't sure what had possessed her mom to come back the first time, but the fact that she had kept Elise thinking her mother might do it again. Her mother was a creature of habit, after all. The stale cigarette-reek of her clothes, the boyfriend she crawled back to every couple of months, the old movie she fell asleep to on the couch after drinking a glass or a bottle or part of a box of wine, it made Elise think that her mother couldn't function if Elise wasn't there.

Elise dove into Fornland like the summer camp she had never attended. She made friends easily and palled around with both the younger and the older girls. She liked sleeping in the Collective—the open space, the mass of girls, the pajama talk—it made her feel like she was a part of something. The first two days when girls asked her what happened to her parents, she said, "My mom is coming back."

"Didn't take you for one of them," Shelly Monark had said. She had been at Fornland for four years and, like someone whose parents had given up on life or their children or their children's lives, gave up on her parents the moment she walked through the door.

"One of what?" Elise asked.

"A believer."

"I'm not." Elise didn't know what Shelly meant, but the disgust in her voice let Elise know it was a bad thing.

"You think your mom's coming back?" Shelly asked.

"Isn't yours?" Elise asked.

Shelly laughed, a sound that didn't come from her stomach, but from the back of her throat, like she choked on it.

"All our moms are coming back," Shelly said. "Some just take longer than others. Like Mal over there." Shelly pointed to a girl who sat on her own at the edge of the table in the common room. She had a vacant stare and unkempt hair. "Her mom is on her way, just a little late is all."

"How late?"

Shelly gave a small smile, a bit twisted. Her hair was frizzy and curly, her eyes were brown and gold. She held up four fingers. Elise tilted her head. "Four what?"

"Years," Shelly said. "Four years."

After that night Elise didn't mention that her mom would soon pick her up. She believed it but didn't say it out loud. After the second week it became a chant in her head before she went to sleep. *She's coming back. She's coming back. She's coming back. She's coming back. She's coming back. She's coming back.* She wanted to whisper it out loud with some certainty because if she couldn't say it out loud, it didn't exist.

Three weeks passed since Elise was dropped off. "I think you need some new clothes," Bernice said. Elise had one set of clothes: white socks, a dark blue shirt, and jeans that had been too big for her but that she grew into. The closest she had gotten to laundry was when she walked into the shower fully clothed. She didn't feel comfortable asking to borrow someone else's clothing; her shirt was ripe with sweat and dust. Her socks hadn't been white for over a week. She had stopped wearing her underwear altogether, even though that was the one garment she could wash, if she wasn't going to be wearing them anyway.

"Where are your colored pencils?" Bernice asked.

Elise didn't look at her. She was ashamed of her dirty clothes and the fact that she had worn her new colored pencils down to the nub once again. She was ashamed because her mother left her on the doorstep of an orphanage and told her she would be back. She felt ashamed because she kept looking at Fornland like a summer camp while all these other girls were stuck there for a lifetime. She had walked around with some sort of snobbish air thinking her mother would walk through the doors at any minute and take her home. She felt ashamed because she had believed her mother.

Bernice went to the Cage, pulled a colorful

yellow pack out, and placed it on the desk in front of Elise.

"You could cry," Bernice said. "Or you couldn't."

The yellow pack with bright red writing looked like sunshine wrapped up on the desk. *Starburst*. Her favorite.

"You may not like it but I think you're going to be here—"

"I would like some new clothes," Elise said. "Please."

That was her initiation into Fornland, a place where Elise learned to divide people into two categories: those that believed their parents would return and those that accepted they wouldn't. Elise had learned to accept her life for what it had become since those days in Bernice's office. Those felt like different lifetimes to Elise. One life ended when she walked into Fornland. A new life started when she walked out of Bernice's office with a fresh pack of Starburst. Another life began when the snow started to fall. Each moment represented a new person she would have to become to survive. Some people called it evolution. She called it acceptance.

She met Abe a few weeks after she had accepted her fate in Fornland. She wore the jeans she came to the boardinghouse in. They were washed. They fit. People crowded around Abe like he was famous; everyone wanted to sit near him. She was drawn to his smile. His raised cheeks, his bright teeth, his shrunken eyes, it was a classic smile she wanted to draw and color in, but her colored pencils were gone, replaced by new clothes and acceptance. He sat and listened to his friend read a story. They laughed at the story. Something about wizards and a griffin, or pumpkin, she wasn't sure. There were four of them listening at the time: Abe, James, Tic-Tac, and Rylie. Two days later, a couple from up north would adopt Rylie. She was stoic and sweet. She didn't talk much but every once in a while she couldn't be stopped.

"Sometimes I like the sound of my voice," Rylie had said. "Other times I don't."

James continued to read. They all looked hypnotized, their eyes stuck on him as he read each word, emphasizing the syllables. Elise wanted to be enraptured like that, by something, by someone, by Abe. His smile kept flashing in her mind. If she couldn't talk to him now she never would. She couldn't accept that.

She crossed the room, each step closer to Abe, each step closer to another new life. There were four large common rooms at Fornland. Two were for the younger kids, places where the corrals and collectives were allowed to hang out together. There was one larger room: SIX-CELLS ONLY written on a sign in red that had dripped off of the page like blood, some sort of metaphor they all could have guessed. Kids in Fornland grew into Six-cells, named for the six beds that filled the rooms instead of the open floor plans filled with as many beds as the boardinghouse could fit such as in the Corral and Collective. The fourth room was a place where six-cells, corrals, and collectives could all hang out together. Six-cells didn't often hang out there but sometimes incentives brought the older kids around the younger ones. Most of the time it was filled with six-cells that just transferred and wanted some time to see their old bunkmates. Everyone called it the Unit. No one knew why. That's where James read and Abe listened.

The incentive for six-cells that night was pizza; many of them came in, grabbed a slice, ignored the corrals and collectives, and walked back to their room. Elise noticed how they all nodded to Abe though. He had just fought Kevin. Everyone knew it. Word of a fight and a crier spread through Fornland faster than a rumor about free candy.

Abe's smile flashed in her head again, his white teeth, his happy face. She crossed the room and sat next to him. She didn't say a word. James didn't stop reading. Tic-Tac might not have noticed.

"It's really good," Rylie said.

"Was there a pumpkin?" Elise asked.

"There's wizards and dragons and—"

"Quiet," Tic-Tac said.

"Do you want me to start back?" James asked.

"Not over," Abe said. "Just from that paragraph."
It was the first time Elise had heard him talk without the interrupting screams of the room. There was a cheery sound, a bright tint in his words. She wasn't ready to introduce herself. She was happy to sit near him, for now.

"This is Abe," Rylie said. "This is Elise."

Abe nodded his head. He smiled a smile directed at her. There was a soft tingle down her spine. She shuffled a bit closer to Abe.

"Hi," Elise said.

It looked like he blushed. James started to read again. Tic-Tac was absorbed right away. Rylie sunk back into her quiet. Elise could feel Abe's warmth drift from his body. She wanted to rest her head on his shoulder.

# LOOSE WAR GAMES

## JAMES

RUMORS OF WAR WERE FILLED WITH BOMBS AND PLANES, tanks and guns, people rising up to flood warmer countries in a tidal wave of migration. When a rumor gained momentum, you could only let it fall over you and hope you didn't drown. War had been different in Fornland when James and Abe were young. The world wasn't frozen and the battle came on a different field.

James sat beneath his bed with a cardboard helmet on his head. The world shook around him, bedposts creaked and scraped along the floor. At least he wasn't covered in piss. When James first arrived in the Corral, Chuck Hayge woke up screaming about the troll beneath his bed that tried to grab him when his eyes were closed. Chuck shook his steel bed frame, rocked the pegs across the tiled floor that filled the room with a piercing screech; he lifted his night shirt, dropped his tighty-whiteys to his ankles, and screamed, "The only thing to keep trolls away is the pee," and proceeded to piss all over his sheets and the floor. James was the only one who didn't stand up on his bed and join in the debauch novelty of urinating all over the Corral floor. Even dogs knew not to piss where they slept. In the morning Chuck mopped up the urine with no memory of the flood. That was a few years ago but sometimes the ridiculous mob mentality came back.

The Corral swayed with the earth's shake. Screams filled the room without restraint; muffled yells faded behind hands; it was worse to show fear than to *be* scared. James crouched beneath his mattress and listened to the room rumble and bedposts scratch; the corral screamed around him. An earthquake was an earthquake was an earthquake, and this earthquake was no bigger than the ones before it. They didn't happen all too often anymore, but when the world began to shake like a box full of marbles, James preferred to listen to the rattle and enjoy the inconsistent movement of the earth.

Abe crouched next to James, a sickly smile on his face. He enjoyed it almost as much as James, or at least it looked like he did. Fake blood made from red watercolors dribbled across Abe's face. James had a similar color splashed along his cardboard helmet and stretched across his stomach.

"You were hit?" Abe asked.

"A flesh wound," James said. No soldier should stop in a fight; any wound was a flesh wound, which to James at the age of nine years old meant anything that didn't hit him in the head, or fake hit him in the head, or take off an arm, or fake take off an arm. The watercolor blood was splattered around the entire Corral. It was along the shaking walls, the stagnant mattresses—some overturned—and the roaming bed frames, not to mention across the bodies and faces of screaming kids. They were in the middle of a massive game of war.

The game had once been played with cards; an easy stamp of high versus low gave a simple matter-of-fact victory in battle. That started to bore everyone. The game then became a mixture of high-low cards and rock-paper-scissors. The corral would separate into equal parts, the card game was played by the two leaders while the others would Rochambeau, then they would average out the winners to see which side claimed victory. Too many kids started to cheat, changing their fingers while the leaders counted, not wanting to let down their generals, their team, or themselves. The leaders would mark the people they counted with red pen so they wouldn't count people twice, but in the end it didn't matter because everyone kept changing their damned rock, paper, or scissors to be a winner. Kids started to fight. Rock turned into fists, paper became slaps, and when kids called out scissors, instead of pretending to cut paper they poked other kids in the eyes.

Then Fornland received the unfortunate donation of a "lifetime supply" of balloons that James and Abe took from the Cage—the locker in the administrator's office that held contraband. War as the corral knew it took shape.

James and Abe were tired of the same arguments and the eventual fights that took place when the corral went to war, the constant cries of "Cheaters!" and the cheaters overall. Instead of complaining, James broke into the Cage, a common enough occurrence for him after his first few years in Fornland, and stole three packs of balloons, each pack filled with seventy-five balloons. He filled them up with a mixture of water and paint donated by a local art supplier; it was a water-based paint that washed off easily. It was probably laced with lead, James thought. He and Abe burst through the door like goddamned Rambo, hitting everything in sight. No one was safe, not a corral, not the walls or the floor. Even the ceiling was splatter-painted with watercolor blood. The screams were a lot less terrified at the time. They sounded more like screeches of unfathomable fun, the type of joyous terror caused by a rollercoaster. Most of Fornland had never been on a rollercoaster.

Water balloons coiled over the room like ocean waves, breaking along the floor of the Corral. The watercolor blood splashed all over everyone as they reenacted a battle from World War I, after having pushed the bed frames and mattresses around the room in an attempt to build their distant version of trenches. If they had the money for Super Soakers they would have used those too; instead the room rained down with watercolor fury, catching corrals in the eyes. The paint dripped from their mouths, their ears, almost stained across their pants—the tragedy of war! Everyone wanted to be America because no one wanted to be the loser. They'd be hard-pressed to know who was on the other side of the war beyond the thought that it had to have been Germany, not because they knew any better. They couldn't imagine a war where Germany was not the *Bad Guy*, was not the *Loser*. If asked who America fought during the Vietnam War or even the war in Afghanistan, most of the corrals would say Germany.

"Do you even know where Vietnam is?" A six-cell once asked a corral.

"Obviously somewhere in Germany," the corral responded. It summed up their knowledge of geography and world history, along with the reason why they didn't bother to claim a country when the balloons started to fall; instead they chose sides.

Rick Tanenbaum had thought it would be funny to piss in his water balloons and mix it with the paint. It wasn't the first time the Corral was covered in someone's piss but it was the first time it had become airborne, the first time someone deliberately showered everyone with it. They all had gotten Tanenbaum back when they made him drink enough cranberry juice that he started to piss red and thought he was bleeding internally. It helped that Abe and James squirted a bit of red paint into Tanenbaum's glass before he drank it. Everyone laughed at him, no one took him to see the nurse, and no one ever pissed inside the balloons again. James chose to ignore the fact that Tanenbaum could have pissed blood because James refused to get the balloons for a week after the incident, which caused uproar in the Corral, but not with James. Tanenbaum had bruised ribs and a black eye for two weeks straight. The benevolence of children didn't stop until James could laugh about Tanenbaum pissing possible blood. No one ever apologized, which made James think it was all square. Tanenbaum was one of the first to leave when the snow started to fall.

The room continued to shake, the war interrupted by the jovial screams quieted. The windows rattled but didn't break. The doors trembled but stayed intact. The world reverberated but never shattered beneath the stress of its own vibrations.

"What does that helmet even protect you from?" Abe asked.

"Stupid people," James said.

"Then you've already lost," Abe said. "And definitely shouldn't be wearing it—'cause you're stupid!"

"I got it," James said.

The rumble of the world ceased. The mattresses stayed upright, the trenches of Corral war intact and ready for the battle to resume. Silence filled the room. Everyone waited for the aftershock. James didn't look out over his bed frame, from behind his mattress, the safety of his trench. He pulled a balloon from the cardboard pouch he had made that matched the cardboard helmet and threw his wannabe grenade into the air.

A splash. A cry. *Ah man*! Balloons sailed through the sky. The battle cries continued.

"You ever want to be in a real war?" Abe asked.

"What would be the point?" James asked.

"Glory? Victory? Money?"

"Death?"

"Can't have glory without death," Abe said.

"And you can't have money with death," James said. "I'd rather have a heartbeat."

Abe took a balloon from his pocket and smashed it on James's cheek. The watercolor blood ran into James's eye and down his neck. It tasted like iron and smelled like a rotten wall. The room trembled again. The screams of fear replaced the yells of joy. Abe hopped over the bed and ran for the other side.

"Victory!" he yelled above the audible anxiety. "We can have victory!"

James wiped the paint from his eye, the sting tingling down his spine and rushing into the back of his head, a place he couldn't touch but wanted desperately to tear out of himself. It went beyond the pain of the blood in his eye and set deep into a lack of understanding. Abe's cries of victory died beneath the screams of fear in the aftershock.

James stood with unstable feet, the blood continuing to drip around his eye. His yell echoed through the rumbled walls. The aftershock screams quieted. He grabbed a balloon from his cardboard pouch and threw as hard as he could at Abe as his body jumped into the trench. The stench of imagined decay and real betrayal was everywhere. Abe fell behind the trench. The balloon sailed through the open sky. The rubber hit the window. The balloon didn't break. The window cracked like a spider web and the crisp sound of the glass crept through the room. The balloon hit the floor; blood sprawled across the tile. The rumble of the walls stopped. The corral stopped, almost as if balloons were caught in the air, everyone unable to answer how James had shattered the window. Abe stood, no longer afraid of the barrage of water balloon retribution. His mouth open. His arms in the air.

"Victory!" Abe said.

The corral laughed. James didn't feel victorious.

# STARTING THE FIGHT

## JAMES

MORE AND MORE KIDS LEFT FORNLAND IN THE RECENT months, when the sky outside was thick with snow. The emptying space was harder to deal with than the crowds James had grown used to. He looked into the empty beds of the Corral and saw the blood stains on the concrete floor.

It was the first broken nose James had ever seen. He couldn't believe how fast and how thick the blood fell from Kevin's nose. It was less like a faucet and more like a shower, sporadic and forceful, splattering onto the concrete floor. Kevin sat with his hands over his face but it didn't stop the blood from seeping through the gaps in his fingers. James thought the first three drops looked like Mickey Mouse, but the rapid fall of blood turned the bleeding illustration from Mickey Mouse to a collection of fresh splatter that would leave a permanent stain.

Abe had thrown one punch and Kevin's nose cracked like a wishbone. The kids stood around and watched the blood pool on the floor of the Corral. They stood on the beds and looked over one another, most of their screams silenced when Kevin dropped to his knees. The ruthless yelled for more, urging Abe to kick Kevin in the ribs, the face, the balls, and get him to scream, but Abe stood with his blood-smeared fist ready to fight if Kevin stood up.

It had started three weeks before. Kevin and James were friends once—not friends, but friendly. Sometimes the classroom door was closed and the kids would have to wait for the teacher of the day to open the door and let them in. James and Kevin told jokes and laughed, stupid jokes that meant nothing.

"What's red and smells like paint?" James asked. "Red paint."

"What's blue and smells like red paint?" Kevin asked. "Blue paint."

The fun and games went too far when James tried to act surprised and offended at one of Kevin's jokes. He grabbed Kevin's shirt and in the process pulled the chain that dangled from Kevin's neck. The chain snapped. Necklaces were one of the few possessions kids were allowed to keep when they arrived in Fornland. Any possession the kids came in with was a connection to a different time, which meant a different world, and at ten years old, James had realized that any time before Fornland was better. James had never heard anyone say they didn't miss their life before Fornland, and they held onto the beautiful dreams of what they thought their lives could have been. *If they thought about life, they would realize that their memories, dreams, and their belief that life was precious before Fornland was a bunch of bullshit,* James thought. When he snapped Kevin's necklace he knew he had stirred the bullshit pot.

"I'm sorry," James said. "It was supposed to be funny."

The chain fell to the floor. The faded gold of the cross glistened in the fluorescent light and hit the ground in silence. Kevin's dark skin flushed red in his cheeks. He was older than James by almost two years. James was a bit shorter but not by much. However, Kevin had the formation of muscles showing on his arms. Kevin's dark eyes and black hair made his red anger look richer and more intense.

"That was from my uncle," Kevin said. "Before he got shot. He was my favorite uncle. It's supposed to look after me."

"It still can," James said. "Easily fixed." James went to pick up the necklace. Kevin pushed him.

"You don't get to touch it," Kevin said. "Ever!"

"I was trying to give it—"

Kevin pushed James again. "Shut it." James hit the wall. "You know you're going to pay for this."

"I don't have any money," James said.

"Good," Kevin said. "Because you can't buy

your way out." Kevin pressed his finger into James's shoulder. His nail pushed through the cushion of his shirt. "You owe me," he said, and stormed off.

James waited another five minutes for someone to open the door, wanting to prove that he wasn't scared or hurt or anxious. He left before anyone came to open the door, ran into Bernice's office, and went to grab a candy bar with some hope that he could salvage the situation with a Snickers. He opened the Cage and ran his hand over the shelves where the Snickers hid but didn't even find the crinkle of a used wrapper.

James tried to avoid Kevin as much as he could. They both slept in the Corral, at least for a few weeks longer. Kevin would soon be twelve and would move into a Six-cell, obtaining some semblance of privacy in their inescapable public world. If James could avoid Kevin for those weeks than he might be able to avoid him long enough to cool down. Every day James tried to avoid Kevin, but Kevin came looking for him. In the hallway he shouldered James into the wall. In the bathroom he snapped a towel on James's back. James's skin swelled up to the size of a baseball. Whatever Kevin did, the pain was bearable but the anxiety of the unknown ate at James. There were stories of kids that had started out with stupid initiations that escalated; one went as far as dropping actual boiled shit onto a kid while he slept and covering him with feathers. As with bullies and rumors, the mind had a way of getting carried away.

James had mapped out different routes to the dining hall, tried to scatter the times he went to the bathroom and used the shower, tried to avoid Kevin at all costs and failed with every attempt. He brushed his teeth in the kitchen to stay out of Kevin's way, but in the dull glow of kitchen light he felt fingers wrap around his hair. His head jerked back. Kevin pulled him to the floor. James's head slammed against the tile. Kevin's fists wrapped around James's hair, pulling hard. James's toothbrush poked him in the back of his throat. He coughed and spat out the toothbrush. He couldn't scream. Kevin released James's hair. He kneeled over James, his knee on top of James's chest. The pressure was heavy on his ribs and his lungs.

"Didn't think you'd get away with it," Kevin said, "did you?"

"I'm sorry," James said with a fractured voice.

"Me too," Kevin said. His fist slammed into James's chin. James tasted pennies. He tried to cover his face but Kevin had pinned one arm to the floor. "I'm sorry you made me do this." One more punch. James lay there, took the punch, tried not to cry, and closed his eyes. Kevin stopped, stood up, and walked away. James wasn't sure why Kevin had stopped but was happy he had. James stayed on the floor and let the cold tile press against his face. He didn't remember falling asleep but woke up with his skin hurting, like he could feel every aching molecule.

"James?" He heard Elise's voice. "Are you okay?" She kneeled over him and screamed for help. James didn't answer. His blood mixed with drooled tooth-paste on the tile. "You're going to be okay," she said. The morning light pulsed around his heavy eyelids.

James woke up in the infirmary. Elise was gone, replaced by Bernice.

"Who did this to you?" Bernice asked.

"I fell," James said. It wasn't some sense of honor that made him think he couldn't tell Bernice. There was some reason he couldn't imagine telling Bernice who had pulled him to the ground, yanked his hair, and pulped his face. His left eye felt swollen but was open. He was surprised he didn't have any broken bones. The gashes along his cheek and the black and blue around his eye weren't as bad as the shattering pain in his head.

There was some hope it was over now, that he and Kevin could go back to the way it was or at least to a form of *nothing* that would be better than this. A pain shot behind James's eye. It was fear, not of Kevin, but of the rest of Fornland. No matter what happened to him, if James snitched he would be defined by the action meant to protect himself, and he would become a bigger target. Kevin would be punished and probably come after James again. The corrals would come after James. The six-cells would come after James. It wasn't a matter of connection, they didn't have to like Kevin—he could be the most hated person in Fornland—but if James snitched he would get it from all angles and he feared that more than the beating he took the night before.

"I heard there was a scuffle with you and Kevin Summers," Bernice said. "That true?"

"I went to the kitchen to brush my teeth. The bathroom was full. I fell."

"I think I know who did it." Abe sat at the edge of the bed.

"Are you going to tell me?" Bernice asked. Abe kept his arms crossed. He wore the same stern look he had when James had woken up. The look somehow fit his face, thin lips and a furrowed brow; that expression didn't often fit on an eleven-year-old's face. "You know what?" she said. "Just take care of it." She walked out of the room. Abe's thin-lipped scowl lessened.

"Why didn't you tell me?" Abe asked.

"I could handle it," James said.

"It shows." Abe lifted the front legs of his chair and rocked back and forth. "You could have said something."

"I wanted to handle it. I thought it would go away."

"It will." The front legs slammed back to the ground. Abe stood up. "Get better."

"Don't do anything," James said. "Okay? At least wait." Abe nodded. He walked out of the room. James's eye recovered, the black and blue faded, and he left the infirmary a few days later. He entered the Corral the same day Kevin was meant to pack up and move into a Six-cell. James walked through the doors and heard clapping. Kevin stood by his bed with his clothes and belongings boxed up and ready to move. His hands slapped together with a large pop.

"Am I supposed to say thank you?" Kevin asked.

James wanted to answer but felt his tongue swell, his mouth desert dry. He wanted to clench his fists and run at Kevin, slam his knuckles into Kevin's cheeks the way Kevin had to him. There was also an overwhelming desire to run away, crawl back onto the kitchen floor, press his cheek to the cool concrete, and cry. He did neither. He stood in silence in the fading echo of Kevin's clapping and tried not to shake.

"You probably should," Abe said.

"This has nothing to do with you," Kevin said.

"I promised I'd wait," Abe said to James. "I didn't promise I wouldn't do anything." Abe kept to himself and didn't like the attention others often gave him. But James and Abe had been close since Abe's first night in the Corral. James helped him once; did Abe think that this was reciprocation? Did he think he needed to repay James at all?

"But you—" James said.

"It's what friends do," Abe said. He walked to Kevin's bed. Abe was shorter than Kevin by almost a hand and a half. He wiped the stuff from Kevin's bed. "Now your problem is with me."

"You're right," Kevin said. "More of the same."

"It's a little different."

The room filled with kids from the Corral, the whispers of a fight spreading through Fornland like wildfire. They stood on chairs and beds, tried to look over one another to see Abe and Kevin toe-to-toe on the concrete floor. Kevin pushed Abe. Abe punched Kevin. One punch. His knuckles drove into Kevin's nose. The room filled with the sickening crunch of cartilage and snapping bone. Kevin's blood spilled onto the floor. The room filled with screams again. James wasn't sure if he was relieved or confused, angry or scared. *What kind of person am I to let my friend fight my battle?* he thought. It had been a long time since he felt so useless.

"It's taken care of," Abe said. He walked out of

the room to the bathroom. James thought it was to wash the blood off Abe's knuckles. The crowd of kids surrounded Kevin. He hadn't stood up.

"We got a crier!" James heard over the screams. Someone whistled. The group started to chant. "Crier! Crier! Crier!" James hoped it was over, but in Fornland you could never be sure.

# SMALL SPACES

## ABE

THE BLANKET OF SNOW OUTSIDE OF FORNLAND MADE IT harder to leave the building. It wasn't because of the snow's height, but the longer the cold and blank-white snow covered the city, the less Abe wanted to leave. Fires throughout San Diego had flattened buildings. The papers Bernice left had become Fornland's last source of heat. The world outside of Fornland once held some luster that all the kids wanted to witness. Now it held destruction.

When Abe and James had moved into a Six-cell, the step up from the Corral, the open space was almost suffocating.

"Pathetic," James said. Bernice let Abe stay in the

Corral until he and James were old enough to move into a Six-cell together. She hadn't done that for anyone, not that Abe knew of in the years he spent in Fornland.

"I know," Abe said. "I've been telling you to get a new hoodie for years." James's hoodie frayed along the seams around his neck. Abe often saw James rub his hands or neck against the seams to push away the threads rather than tear them away. It had a banana slug on it, with big, goofy, googly eyes, and a stupid grin. He had worn it for years and started to grow into it. Just as he grew into the dark gray and white-flecked sweatshirt it was time to get rid of the tawdry thing. James smoothed his hands over the banana slug, swiping at the moldy scent and years of grime.

"Not what I meant," James said.

"It should have been," Abe said.

James looked around the Six-cell. To Abe the confinement felt liberating. He had never thought an enclosed space would make him feel better but the lack of open space meant a lack of beds, it meant the lack of other kids' eyes on him all the time. He was sure he didn't have the desire for seclusion when he was younger, before Fornland. It wasn't that hard to imagine himself raising his hands in the air around his parents in a desperate attempt for them to look at him, notice him, even. That wasn't privacy, that was loneliness, and there was a difference. In the past six years, the Six-cell became the mark of growing up.

There were two rungs: Six-cell and Exit. The Exit was exactly how it sounded. It was a celebration when a group of kids came of age and went out into the world. There was cake if they got to it early enough. There was a yellow banner with large red block letters: Happy Exit! One was a quiet move, the other a battle cry, all the exes ready to run out and war with the world, take it head on, even if fear rattled their eyeballs. Abe didn't want out in the world, he just wanted to get out of Fornland and into a place of his own, even at twelve years old.

"This, man," James said. "This hole that we're in now."

James was one for space, even if not the space of the Corral. He liked the open air and the windows. It wasn't a secret. A few times Abe saw him sitting on Johann's bed beneath one of the long stretches of dirty windows. That wasn't allowed in the Corral, an unwritten rule among the boys. When a bed is the only possession they had, they guarded it like a mother bird. They decorated and protected their beds, but then grew up, gave the bed up, and moved on to somewhere else. Maybe James had understood that before.

Abe found James on Johann's bed, whose name was really John but thought it sounded better in Swedish. James's legs were kicked out, swinging over the floor. His head was pressed against the wall and he stared through the crusty window.

"There's a lot out there," James had said. "Look at it." Abe didn't feel right going onto another kid's bed without an invite, even if it was Johann's.

"I can see the crappy window from here," Abe said.

"There's more than that," James said.

"I believe you," Abe said.

When Abe arrived in Fornland, he felt like he had developed a superpower, where he could look at someone's face and know what they longed for, the one desire they had in life. Some people wore it on their sleeves like marker stains: *I want to see my family again*, or *I want to be a part of a family*. Those were the kids that either made the most friends to gain some sense of connection with a world that never wanted them, or spent the first six months refusing to talk to anyone because they were certain their parents, grandparents, brother, sister, cousin, uncle, aunt, or mom's best friend would pick them up.

Other kids were harder to read but still had their tells, somewhere in the corner of their smiles or in the lost light of their eyes. The joyless kids often had the same desire to leave Fornland, but in some dramatic exit without clinging to the hope of what was outside the walls of the boardinghouse. If they graduated to exes at all, they were the ones who put on a grand display, popping out their middle fingers, filled with shouts and ball grabs as if the motion were unique to them, even though they got it from the guy who had Exed the year before, and so on.

It wasn't as if they were locked inside the boardinghouse at all times, or at all, without the ability to walk outside and see the city, explore, or leave. It was a secret that they all knew; Arnis Karfson had done it. Abe and James listened through Bernice's door. Arnis was fifteen at the time, but he looked twenty-two and acted thirteen, in that delicate balance of immaturity and thinking he knew better.

"I'm leaving," Arnis said.

"When will you be back?" Bernice asked.

"I won't be."

"Where are you going?"

"Away."

"I can see that," Bernice said. Abe and James felt like spies as they listened in on the meeting of a secret club—them, Bernice, and Arnis. "Any thought on where you'll end up? You should have a plan."

"I don't need one," Arnis said. "What I need is out of this place."

"You can't wait a few years?" Bernice asked.

"No."

"Do you think it's going to be easy?"

"No."

"Why are you going?"

"I don't have to tell you."

It was on the back of Kelly Rippa's Exit. Arnis used to follow her around like an alley cat; the moment she showed him any interest, he turned away. She hadn't been back in six weeks. No one ever came back.

"I'm sorry to hear that, Arnis. You'll be missed. I expect your bed to be open by the end of the night?"

"That's it? But—yes. It's open."

"If you find yourself with a phone you can call

this number . . . if you need help. You remember Kelly, I'm sure."

Abe and James cut from the door and watched Arnis walk out of Bernice's office, pick up his bag that looked too small for a boy his size, and walk out of Fornland forever. After he left, rumors spread that he was adopted, arrested, picked up as a bouncer for one of the local strip clubs, and drafted into the Arena Football League. No one really knew what happened to him after he left, though.

"It's not a prison," Bernice said. Abe and James looked at each other. Bernice hadn't left her office. They didn't know she was speaking to them. "I know you boys are there."

They walked to the doorframe. Bernice sat behind her desk. She looked elegant, without the usual frazzled hair and tired eyes. The door framed her in her office like a picture out of a book she read to them.

"It's not a prison," she said. "You can come and go anytime you want."

"You didn't try to stop him," Abe said.

"There's a world out there that's worse than this," Bernice said. "It's your choice if you want to go through it without help."

"Why didn't you try to stop him?" James asked.

"No one wants to be here," Bernice said. "Nothing would make me happier than to be out of a job, to live in a world where this bitch of a position didn't exist. But the world can be cruel and awful—"

"So can this place," Abe said.

"Sure," Bernice said. "But it's a hell of a lot better than what you'd find out there. I'm not saying this is grand, but it's the best I can do and it's the best you're going to get for a while, at least until your Exits."

"Will he be back?" James asked.

Abe couldn't understand why James cared. He didn't know Arnis. People got tired fast with his constant talk about *escaping*, as if he had mapped an escape route hidden underneath his mattress. In the end, Arnis picked up his stuff and walked out the front door.

"Arnis?" Bernice asked. "I doubt it. I hope he makes it."

"Makes what?" Abe asked.

"To whatever he's looking for," Bernice said.

The kids who wanted to leave, who had an undying urge to escape hidden within the twitches of their fingers and cuts of their cracked lips, didn't think much of life beyond their exit. They talked about and thought about how life would be so much better outside of Fornland, but no one ever had a plan how, like Arnis. It was one of the reasons Abe fell in with James. Everyone else's need was apparent, singular. James was more complicated; Abe couldn't tell what it was James looked for, and in truth, he was sure James didn't know either.

In the comfortable closeness of their new Six-cell, James seemed uncomfortable.

"We've spent, like, six years waiting," James said. "This is us growing up, right?"

"Sure," Abe said. "Why not."

"All I'm saying is we waited all that time and anticipated all that time to move into a small room with six. It's pretty anticlimactic. There's got to be something more, right?"

"There is," Abe said. He threw a candy bar at James. It was a king-sized Kit-Kat, the type that could make you sick if you ate the whole bar too quickly. It had made them sick once. Abe had once taken two from a liquor store. *Why share when we can each have one?* They ran to the park and sat beneath a tree. They snapped apart each division. James bit off the top layer first, then nibbled on the edges each time. Abe broke a division, snapped it in half, and stuffed each piece into his cheeks before he chewed. Abe finished his bar in two minutes and fourteen seconds flat. James finished a little more than half before a squirrel jumped from the tree they sat beneath, stole the remainder of the chocolate crisp, and ran up to distant tree branches with the chocolate crunch and wrapper falling around them.

Even with only half the candy bar finished, James felt sick later that day, and so did Abe. They missed dinner and stayed holding their stomachs in the Corral. It had been worth it.

"Did you—?" James asked.

"Not from me," Abe said. James raised his eyebrows. "It's a moving-in present I think. Guess you don't need to steal any Snickers today."

"Why would she do that?" James asked.

"She got sick of running out of candy, I'm sure."

James sat next to Abe. They opened the wrappers. Abe broke each division in two before he shoved the pieces into his cheeks. James ate the top of the division before he nibbled at the remainder. He checked the window and the doorway.

"If a squirrel rushes through here," Abe said, "I think him grabbing your candy will be the least of our problems." Chocolate smeared over James's mouth. Abe wiped his face to make sure the same hadn't happened to him. "Works for you?"

# STORIES TOLD

## JAMES

THE ENDLESS WINTER STARTED FOR FORNLANDERS WHEN THEY first stepped through the doors, not realizing what their lives would become. No one expected an actual winter. James had told Marcus stories shortly after Marcus arrived.

"I'd love to be in a story," Marcus had said.

"Me too," James told him. "I always wanted to be a hero."

"Me too!" Marcus said. They used to sit on Marcus's bed while James read the hard words and Marcus pointed to the pictures. His favorite was *The Little Prince*.

Marcus was five when he first entered Fornland.

James had moved into his Six-cell. Marcus was a crier. Most kids stopped crying after their first five days, after they made their first friend, after they learned the food was better than the food they ate on the street or at home. When whispers of a crier flittered through the rooms of Fornland, it was a big deal. It meant the same kid cried every night without fail for longer than ten days.

There were three people James remembered labeled as criers. James would have been labeled a crier too if he had understood the truth: his parents weren't coming back. Instead, for two weeks he lay in bed at night and watched the street lamps shine through the open windows like searchlights at a prison. The dust floated through the light while people slept, until the night Chuck Hayge screamed about trolls and flooded the Corral with piss. James had been lucky. Marcus hadn't been lucky. There were no screams or lights to distract him from his tears, or to distract the corrals from him.

Criers were easily ostracized, seen as different.

The Corral was the first test of a Fornlander's strength. If you spent more than ten days crying, then you were weak. No corral cared how a kid dealt with his emotions as long as it didn't affect anyone else. If a kid cried, it affected everyone.

On the twelfth day, James went to the small library and pulled out a ratty copy of *The Little Prince*. It was flat and easy to hide. Stuffed animals didn't last long in the Corral. They were stolen, heads torn off, and stuffed beneath the sheets. Contraband was never given up to Bernice; other kids took it. Whether it was re-appropriated or it just disappeared, someone had to earn the right to his contraband. If it was taken, that person hadn't earned it. James wouldn't waste his efforts on something that would be taken from Marcus, showing him that he had become the lowest nibble on the food chain. No stuffed animals, no photographs— the photos wouldn't have been of Marcus anyway. James took the book.

The Corral was empty when James walked in.

He had been a six-cell for almost four months now. He no longer had to fear the acrid perfume of piss draped across his sheets. He shared a room and a bunk with Abe. James slept on the bottom bunk because he was too lazy to climb a ladder every night. When James walked into the Corral, Marcus was alone on his bed. The room looked like a war hospital. How had James never noticed it before? The beds were spread equidistant, all covered with the same sheets, the corners stuffed neatly between the mattress and the frame. Marcus's bed hadn't been made; the sheets were not stretched over the mattress to hide all the creases that indicated the linens hadn't been washed in the past month. James sat next to Marcus. Marcus stared at his feet. He wore Velcro shoes with faded Spiderman faces on the sides.

"You're the crier," James said. Marcus didn't move, didn't blink, he might not have even breathed.

"I just mean—" James said. "I heard you're

having a tough time. I know what it feels like to be new." It wasn't a lie, but everyone knew what it was like to be new to Fornland. No one was born into Fornland and everyone had to learn how to fit in. It was easier for some than others. It was easier for those that had felt lost and alone most of their lives; they learned to be chameleons early on, to blend into the walls if they had to. The fact that Marcus spent the last however-many days crying meant he didn't come from a family of drug users or physical abusers. Criers tended to come from homes taken by surprise, an unforeseen occurrence or a misunderstanding of a public incident taken too far and never corrected, like when a father beats a guy half to death with his bare fists, blood splattered across his face and skin as the guy lies motionless on the asphalt of downtown San Diego, because the guy groped the irate father's son. The man went to the hospital, the father went to jail, and the kid got sent to Fornland. *Justice my ass.*

That was the rumor of Marcus's fate, why he

couldn't stop crying, the guilt he probably felt over his father's arrest while he was stuck here, as if it was his fault some sick bastard wanted to touch him. It wasn't Marcus's fault he was one of the few kids in Fornland who had a father who cared enough to protect his son with his life, or spend life in prison to do so. Whether or not the rumor was true, that's what everyone chose to believe about Marcus. It didn't make him any less of a target.

Marcus took quick, silent breaths. The sunlight beamed through the windows and cast shadows beneath the beds where the trolls used to hide.

"I found this," James said. He placed the book on the bed. "In the Cage," he lied. "I'm pretty sure it belonged to you."

Marcus looked at the book. He rubbed his tiny fingers over the cover. He shook his head. His hair was short and brown.

"Are you sure?" James asked. "One of the corrals told me you talk in your sleep. You had said something about a book." James didn't feel remorse from the lie. It was about Marcus; it was about getting Marcus to fit in, at least to a degree that he could move on. The times when he could help a Fornlander were the closest James ever felt to being a hero, but even in those moments he never felt like the hero he wanted to be. Heroes saved lives, not just from burnt buildings, but also from decimated character.

Marcus shook his head again. He couldn't be convinced about the book. James didn't blame him. It wasn't the most convincing lie James had told.

"You ever want to be a ninja?" James asked. "I did. When I was about your age I thought I was a ninja." The light from the window glowed brighter and the shadows beneath the beds receded. "I dressed in black and tried to hide in closets and stick to walls. Do you know karate? I don't. I didn't then either. But I thought if I hid well enough, I wouldn't have to know karate."

"I miss my dad," Marcus said. It was the first

time he looked up from his shoes. The faded Spiderman faces swung with his feet.

"It's a lot harder to hide here than other places."

"It's my fault he is gone. It's my fault I'm here."

"From what I heard, your dad loved you," James said. "That's more than some can say. Sounds like he was a real ninja." James rubbed his hand over the book. "Like this guy here. It makes sense why he would have given it to you. He wanted to remind you to be strong, smart, and get out of this place. Plus, this way you would always have something to keep you busy." James hoped it sounded like something Marcus's father would say, something a father who would beat the life out of a man would say to his son. "Don't count down the days, right? Then you waste your time worried about what has been."

Marcus looked at the book. "It does sound like him." It was the first smile James had seen from Marcus. His feet continued to swing in the light. He opened the book to a painting of a sprawling desert. "Deserts get less than ten inches of rain a year. My dad taught me that. He taught me the days of the week, and how to count and, and—"

"And how to be like a ninja," James said. "Keep it between your mattress and the frame. You're a ninja. Don't forget it."

"He taught me to be an explorer," Marcus said.

"Even better."

Marcus picked up the book and held it like he would his father. The closest tangible object he had to his father, even if it wasn't real. When their lives became too hard to survive, it was more important to create a life worth living. It was the first time James understood how willing people were to give up a sense of themselves for a sense of who they would rather be, for a sense of what they would rather have.

After six months, Bernice called Marcus into her office. James heard the story through the string of whispers.

"Shanked," a dark-haired boy said.

"Bled out," a tall, light-eyed girl said.

No one knew what actually happened and no one asked. Marcus cried for five more days. He held onto the book. No one called him a crier. Everyone left him alone, holding onto the twilight cover and counting days.

*Sometimes it is easier to lie to yourself,* James thought. How long had he been doing it? Lies were easier to swallow in this place. It felt good to make some aspect of their lives easier.

# THE NECESSITY
# OF ESCAPE

## ABE

ABE WALKED THROUGH THE DOOR AND SLAPPED HIS HAT ON his thigh. "Okay," he said. Frost fell to the floor. "Let's get out of this hellhole." For two months Abe had tried to find a way out of the cold, ever since they burned the last of Bernice's papers. The room had looked the same but cleaner, spotless, with no clutter to mask the room that once felt cramped but actually had plenty of space. Whatever warmth they had left went with the last remnants of Bernice's reports and kids' scattered histories of child services.

The window next to James's bed was iced from the outside in.

"Remember how the border patrol used to know us by name?" James said. "We've never been allowed into Tijuana; I doubt they'll start now."

"Better idea," Abe said. He raised his eyebrows, he wanted James to ask the question, but James sat silently. They had divided up their missions. Abe would try to find a way out of Fornland, a place to survive in what had become a bitter wasteland. James would keep whatever was left of Fornland going, including whoever was left. James tried to wipe away the ice from the window but instead spread condensation around the glass.

The snow had held promise, for a moment. Abe, Elise, and James had stood outside the doors of the boardinghouse. The sky filled with the riotous gray of endless clouds. Elise shivered but didn't go inside. Abe wrapped his arms around her. James lit a cigarette; he said it made him feel older, wiser, in charge of his own life, even if he couldn't buy the pack himself. A single snowflake landed on the pack of cigarettes, another landed on the tip of Elise's nose.

James noticed the unique outline of the ice crystals, the geometric spears that circled its outer ring before it melted. He dropped his cigarettes. Abe and Elise watched the flake melt on her skin. They stood beneath the flurry; being alone on the street made them feel the world stormed just for them—their own personal blizzard—and they had never seen anything more beautiful.

Abe and Elise's initials had been dug into the sidewalk at the corner of the street. The cement had been wet long before the snow fell. Elise kept Abe from stepping in it. Instead he dug his finger in and carved out their first letters side by side.

"It's like having an address," Elise said. "Or something." The initials were on the corner close to Fornland. She looked at them every day when she passed; Abe did too. Sometimes she would just go outside to make sure they were there.

"Where are you going?" Abe asked.

"Nowhere," she would say, and he would see her strolling to the corner with a wide smile on her face, almost skipping on the way back, her own private ritual.

When the snow fell heavy over the city, Elise looked out the window over the blanket of white. "They're gone," was all she said. She whispered it into the glass, looking out the window of one of the common rooms, as the frost covered the squares. There was always a moment when any Fornland kid realized that things weren't forever, that even when they found a glint of happiness, it might not last. Abe knew that was Elise's moment. Parents left, friends left, seasons changed, even in San Diego, but sometimes they could carve out a decent enough life amidst the changing landscape to be happy for a minute. The hardest part was watching that minute end.

Abe didn't say a word. He didn't grab his coat or put on shoes. He walked outside in white socks that pressed into the snow and absorbed the cold wetness. He didn't wrap his hands around his arms or warm his chest. The snow fell but not hard. He looked up to the window and saw Elise staring, searching for their lost initials. He stood over the exact spot their initials had sat side by side, looked up, and waved. Her head turned in a way that told Abe she didn't realize he had left her side.

Abe had taken a broomstick from the lobby of Fornland and held it close. He dug the end of the handle into the snow as deep as it would go. He carved an A and an E warped together: Æ. When he was done he looked up to the window. Elise's face was almost hidden by the frost, but he could see her smile. Every day that their initials were covered by the snow Abe would go back to that spot and reclaim their slice of sidewalk. Those days were almost over.

In the chill of James and Abe's Six-cell, James finally asked. "What is it?"

Abe wanted to return to the feeling of the flurry, when for a few brief moments he felt like the world was on their side, like life didn't have be so hard all of the time. He knew James hadn't smoked a cigarette since. He knew Elise wanted their initials to last forever.

"A boat," Abe said. "Let's get out of here."

Abe hadn't tried to leave Fornland since he was eleven years old. The sun had been hot, the waves friendly, and he had found himself the unwanted center of attention.

One day he'd been out exploring. The waves crashed against the beach and the sun reflected off of the sand. Abe's bag was heavy in his hand. The ocean smelled warm and fresh. People littered the beach in bathing suits, their skin tan. Surfboards cut through the water, white foam splashed into the air. This was life outside Fornland and he wanted to sink into it. The night before, he'd spent the night along the boardwalk of Pacific Beach. The bars were loud and obnoxious until two in the morning, when people fell out the doors onto the sidewalk and into the street, plowed through one another, and sang their way home. Abe had walked along the boardwalk with his bag, the sand crunching beneath his feet. One night outside of Fornland wasn't so bad.

It had been three weeks since he made Kevin's nose bleed. He'd wanted to help James, was all. Fornland changed after Abe's fight with Kevin. Kids started to watch Abe. Stared at him even. James and Elise were the two people that stayed the same.

When the fight ended, all James had said was, "Thank you." Elise didn't mention the fight but wrapped Abe's knuckles in bandages.

"They aren't hurt," Abe told her.

She shushed him. "It's a precaution."

The rest of the boardinghouse looked at Abe in a way he didn't understand. All he wanted was to not be looked at. He'd spent so much time when he was younger trying to get attention. Once he finally had it, he wasn't sure what to do with it. He'd packed his bag the previous afternoon and walked out the door. He didn't tell James. He didn't tell Elise. He didn't tell Bernice. He didn't want to. He didn't think he needed to. They'd figure it out.

"Hey, kid," a woman called out. "Buy you a Coke?"

It was Bernice. She wore a bikini, the contours of her body changed with the flash of her skin beneath a black two-piece rather than the slathered and wrinkled patterned dresses and sweatshirts she often wore. Water glistened off her body. Abe wasn't sure if it was sweat or the shore. The bag was getting heavy. It was midafternoon and he hadn't eaten yet. He had spent most of the morning catching up on the sleep he didn't get when the jovial drunkards had slipped down the street. He nodded his head.

"Robbie," she said. A man with flowers on his swim trunks and hair on his stomach turned. He held a beer in his hand that he tried to hide from Abe. "This is one of the boys I told you about."

"Which—wait," Robbie said. "The knuckler? Heard it was a nice shot. But you didn't hear that from me." Robbie winked in that condescending way that adults often did to kids when they weren't sure what to say. At the same time Abe liked the compliment and felt his cheeks go red.

"Enjoying the beach?" asked Robbie.

"I was just going to get him a Coke," Bernice said. Robbie took a sip of his beer. He probably thought Abe had seen worse things than a grown man drinking in public. He was right. "I'll be back."

"Every good fighter should get a reward," Robbie said.

"Stop it," Bernice said. She brushed Robbie's arm and smiled.

Abe and Bernice walked along the boardwalk in silence. They passed two liquor stores, an ice cream man, and a Burger King, all of which sold Coke, all of which Bernice didn't glance at. She walked into an open patio with wooden picnic tables and sporadic checkered umbrellas. She sat down; Abe followed. The waitress came by.

"Two Cokes, please," Bernice said.

"Anything else?" the waitress asked. Bernice kept

her eyes on Abe. Abe watched Bernice. He squinted. She had a soft, half-smile, and her eyes were a bit tired.

"No, thank you," Bernice said. "Just the Cokes." The waitress walked away. Seagulls cawed in the background. People chattered along the boardwalk and the patio but Bernice didn't say a word. It became a battle of wills, Abe thought. Whoever spoke first, lost. He didn't have to speak. He could stare at her in silence for as long as she could. He didn't need her to make him feel guilty for leaving. It was his choice. She had said Fornland wasn't a prison—people were free to go if that's what they wanted, and that's what Abe wanted.

"Robbie's my fiancé," Bernice said. "He's a lawyer. Helps me out now and again, but works long hours. Not unlike me. He's a nice guy though. We've been together for a while."

Abe didn't want the confusion in his mind to spread across his face. He didn't understand why she was talking about Robbie and not about why he had his bag with him. It was obvious he had left and hadn't talked to her about it. He thought she'd at least mention it.

"Remember that face you made when you first got to Fornland?" Bernice asked. The waitress put the Cokes on the table. They were glass bottles with straws that floated in the soda and poked out of the narrow lips. Bernice said thank you and the waitress walked away. "You're making that same face now. That want-to-be-tough look that looks more like you ate a sour lemon." Abe relaxed his face but crossed his arms. "How about you talk to me."

"About what?" Abe asked.

"Surfing," Bernice said. "You ever been?"

"Surfing?" Abe asked.

"Robbie's a great surfer. Sometimes he goes out before work, if he can. He's been doing it for years. You want him to teach you how? You seem to have time on your hands, and maybe a pair of shorts in your bag." Abe's jeans already felt slick and dirty from the sand and the sweat. The days were warm but the nights were cold, and he had worried more about the nights than the days when he walked out of Fornland. He hadn't thought about food or showers. He ended up like the kids that most annoyed him, the ones who cared more about leaving than what would happen after they left.

He told himself he had a plan: make it to Los Angeles. The longer he sat with Bernice, the more he realized that, one, he didn't have an idea what would happen after that, and two, it was a bad plan to begin with. His dad had been a musician once. Abe thought maybe, if he made it to LA, he could run into one of his dad's friends and they'd help him out for a minute. But he was eleven and had never met any of his dad's friends from LA, which put Abe into the first category of kids in Fornland, the ones that always looked for some deeper connection. All that did was piss him off.

"What do you think?" Bernice asked.

"I've never been surfing," Abe said.

"Where were you taking that bag?"

"For a walk," Abe said. "It needed some air." He took a sip of the Coke. It fizzed and bubbled on the way down his throat.

"How far were you thinking about walking?"

The waves continued to crash in behind Bernice. Abe watched a surfer roll beneath and pop out the other side.

"Until I find what I'm looking for," Abe said.

"Do you know what you're looking for?"

The sea breeze filled the silence between them. Bernice sipped her Coke. Abe wasn't looking for something specific, maybe not even tangible, but he wanted away from the watching eyes.

"You tell James?" Bernice asked. "Or Elise? They could have helped you find it, maybe."

"I don't owe them anything," Abe said. "And they owe me nothing."

"James didn't really talk to anyone before you came around. Elise was too busy thinking her mom would come back any second. It's not about owing someone either way." She sipped her Coke. It was almost gone, filled with sporadic slurps. "It seemed like you guys were good friends is all. Thought you would have at least told one of them."

"What's the hard-on you have for James?"

"Despite the fact that I don't have a hard-on at all, indulge me. What do you mean?"

"Why do you treat him so different from everyone else? We all see it. He's the only one with a key to the Cage."

"That was supposed to be his and my secret."

"It was, but it wasn't hard to figure out when he kept coming back with more and more candy. Even if he stole it all, you would have noticed when that much was missing, unless you were letting him have it."

"James came in like you did, like most of the kids did. I've seen how you look at the rest of the kids in there. You know they all have some bigger dream about the place, some hope they hold on to about family or running away, like that bag of yours. I hadn't taken you for a runner. I took you to be more like James. He came in without fear or sadness but with some air of . . . acceptance, I guess. He sat in the same chair you sat in and just accepted life. That's someone I want to watch out for. I thought you were the same, or at least similar. I guess I was wrong."

"Maybe you were." Abe didn't want her to be wrong. He wanted be strong. He wanted to be brave. He wanted to be the fireman that he had pretended to be when he and James would fight fake fires. It was hard to fall short of the person he hoped to be. "I got tired of all the eyes on me."

Bernice slurped the empty air of her Coke bottle. The straw was stuck between her lips and rolled around the base of the glass in search of leftover droplets.

"They're ready to follow you," Bernice said.

"Where?" Abe asked.

"Anywhere. They look at what you did to Kevin as a sign of something bigger, kid. Like you're a natural born leader."

"Not really."

"Yes, really. Where you going to lead them? You going to disappear or you going to stick around? I'm not sure James will find another friend like you. Elise will be heartbroken. You know she's tender. They both are."

"I have nowhere to lead anyone," Abe said.

"There comes a point in your life when you get let down so many times that you just don't want to bother with people anymore. Don't add to that, not to James. Not to Elise. Don't let people do that to you. Promise."

And then it floated out of his mouth before he knew he said it. "I promise." It was the first step he took in the direction of something bigger than drooling himself to death like his father. Bernice cared about him. She cared about Fornland. It was the best the boardinghouse had, and at that moment Abe wouldn't change it. They stood up. Bernice went back to Robbie. Abe turned towards Fornland. He turned around to wave at Bernice, but she walked with Robbie closer to the water. Somehow, even when she left Fornland with a few hugs and a paper trail, Abe never felt like she'd let him down. He made the promise that he wouldn't let that happen to himself, to Elise, to James. He wanted to be more like James and accept life.

Abe walked into the Corral. He put his bag on his bed. The springs wobbled.

"Welcome back," James said. Elise ran into the Corral. Some boy shouted that she wasn't supposed to be there.

"Shut your face, Geoff!" she screamed. "You asshole." She stormed towards Abe. "You didn't even tell me—us." She slapped Abe's arm before hugging him and digging her head into his shoulder.

"I didn't go far," Abe said. They left the moment behind like a separate dream they were happier not to take with them.

# A NEW BEGINNING

## JAMES

THE GOLD-PLATED PLAQUE GLISTENED IN THE COLD.

DEDICATED TO THE BRAVERY AND PEACEFUL SOUL OF SAMUEL S. FORNLAND, MAY HIS SPIRIT BLESS ALL——

Ice crept over the remaining words, cracked and unreadable.

Abe reached for the door. James stopped him. He shambled down the stairs and tripped on the broken steel frame.

"A boat needs people," James said. The boardinghouse looked like a picture James once saw on a billboard. *We buy terrible things,* the billboard had said. James wanted to try to sell his memories, make a few bucks, and get the hell out of town, but by *terrible things* the company meant crappy houses. The thought to sell Fornland had come and gone but never in earnest. The brick crumbled. The roof was punctured with holes. That was from the outside. *Now the only thing holding up the exterior of the boardinghouse is the ice*, James thought.

"We have people," Abe said. "You." Abe slapped James on the shoulder. "Elise and me." He reached for the door once more but the handle wouldn't turn. The cheap metal had frozen, as they knew it would eventually, but James had hoped it wouldn't.

The boardinghouse was too big to heat even if the remainder of rowdy abandonees had the means to heat a single room anymore. The papers were gone, gasoline was a memory, and the only wood left in the city was stuck in frozen trees or nailed to the buildings that hadn't yet burned. James and Abe were lucky—if anyone could call it that—because of how long they had been in Fornland.

They had shared the Six-cell with four others,

until Thom and Wes bolted for Columbia. When they hadn't shown up one random night James figured they had got caught at the border and shoved into a detention center, similar to Fornland but with less space, which in the cold meant chockfull of body heat. Maybe it wouldn't be so bad.

"Why Columbia?" James had asked Thom.

"Ever heard of snow in Columbia?" Thom asked.

"Ever hear of snow in San Diego?" James asked.

"Columbian girls," said Wes. "And everyone's heard of Columbian snow. They sell it in baggies and you sniff it." Wes winked.

"If you want cocaine you can go shove your face in the blizzard and inhale," James said. "Probably numb your brain the same."

That was three months ago, around the midpoint between the first snow and now, when the fires burned bright enough to keep the constant worry of frozen fingers away. If half the city burned, the other half would freeze.

Abe tried to turn the frozen handle.

"Let's wait," James said.

"For the building to fall?" Abe asked.

"Let's wait till the rest get back."

*The rest.* He meant those that lingered around the boardinghouse like zombies because they were too small to run away, too scared to run away, or, like James and Abe, had nowhere to run to.

"And that would help because?"

Charlotte. He could count on one hand how many times he'd spoken to her beyond the bounds of a head-nod or hello. He could count it on one finger.

Months after the snow had fallen, James had been wandering around Fornland with blankets. The roof in the central hall had collapsed. There were fewer girls than guys for most of his time in Fornland, but when the kids started to run, it was the guys who scattered first and most. It meant a number of blankets suddenly freed up. James came across Charlotte sitting in her Six-cell.

"Cold," he had said.

"Yeah," Charlotte said.

He came and sat down next to her. He rubbed his hand through his hair, and smeared the snowy streaks into water. His black bangs ran back over his eyebrows.

More girls stayed behind, for whatever reason. *For the same reason they went to the bathroom in pairs*, James thought, *maybe, safety in numbers.*

"Blanket?" James asked.

"Yeah," she said.

He handed her the blanket. Some blankets he had taken from the cupboards littered around the house. Others he and Abe had "liberated" from one of the linen stores after the snow started to fall. James and Abe agreed that they had spent enough time in Fornland, as children and teens, to know that it was always cold inside those walls. They spent a long time promising themselves they wouldn't die inside Fornland before and they'd be goddamned if they would let the cold take them now.

"Okay," James had said. He started to walk out

of Charlotte's Six-cell, wanted to wander into the snow to cool off. If she warmed him that much, he should spend more time around her, where the air wouldn't sneak between his ribs and stab him with cold pinpricks.

He had noticed Charlotte when she walked into Fornland two years before—he had been almost fourteen. He noticed her eyes, hidden behind her hair that hung around her face, and the stuffed walrus clasped between her crossed arms. Her hair had been pink at the time, and shined like she had taken crappy highlighters to it, which James found out she had after he overheard a conversation between Charlotte and Elise. It wasn't her pink hair that James noticed the most though, it was the way she hid her eyes behind the pink that made them stand out even more. They were bright green at a time when green was everywhere around the city. The trees were still alive; the bushes, when not dried to a dead brown and covered in flames, were also alive. Parks had blossomed flowers and nowhere in the city, unless stuffed somewhere in an ice-skating rink that James didn't know existed, was there snow. How many people noticed her eyes then? Now it was hard not to notice. Her eyes reminded him of a past that everyone wanted to hold on to, before the streets were covered in white, the buildings in white, the trees, white. But that's what her eyes reminded him of: the warm open park before the storm. When he offered her a blanket her hair was no longer pink. It had been white for months.

"It's ironic," she said.

James turned around. "What?"

"My hair," she said. "It's ironic because of the snow."

James pressed his hand to the doorframe and leaned in.

"That's not ironic," he said. "That's white snow on the ground and white in your hair."

"How is it not ironic?"

"Standing in a blizzard but burning to death, that's irony. Hating children and dying during childbirth, that's irony. Loving someone so much that you can't live without them so then you kill them, that's—"

"I get it," she said.

"I don't think I do."

James had walked away from the door. He'd known he should have just agreed with her.

James watched Abe slam his shoulder against the door, then pull away and slam his shoulder harder. The layer of snow on the outside quieted the thud.

"Shouldn't we wait for Elise?" James asked.

Abe tried to pull the door again. His face began to turn from flush white to hold-your-breath red. He didn't look at James as he pulled at the door, slamming his shoulder against it. Pulled. Slammed. Pulled, until he was out of breath.

"Why aren't you helping?" Abe asked.

"We need more people," James said.

"I know where Elise is," Abe said. "I wouldn't leave without her."

"But everyone else?"

"We don't owe them shit, man."

"I never said we owe anyone anything, but it's not like we have anywhere to go."

"So you'd rather bring them all with us to nowhere?"

A crash thundered and jolted the boardinghouse. Snow snuck through the tarp they had placed over the hole. The scent of acrid smoke sifted through the air.

"Couldn't be worse," James said.

Abe pulled against the door once more. It opened. Flames danced over the buildings a short distance way.

"Hamez," Abe said. Abe was the only one who called James that, and James was never sure why. But it reminded James of when he was young and his mom would call him by a similar-sounding name. Abe squeezed James's shoulder and continued, "It could always be worse."

# OLD ROOMS AND COLD FACES

## JAMES

WHEN THE REMAINDER OF FORNLAND RETURNED FROM foraging, they found James and Abe pushing snow through the hallways and cavernous rooms as if the snow were a novelty, their snow angels unique, like they brought the snow in to save it from melting. One by one, James and Abe threw snowballs, chunks of ice, and, at one point, stale and frozen shoes at the kids that walked through the door. Each kid had gone out in search of food, heat, clothing, or just to escape the boardinghouse for a minute. Fornland was a place for the abandoned, the unloved, the forgotten, as Bernice had called some of them.

There were less than one hundred of them left. Abe seemed to know all of their names. James remembered their faces, but as Fornland became smaller, the majority of them became closer—the family none of them ever had and always needed.

Abe called them into the Collective. The Corral had frozen over and the remainder of the boys had taken shelter in the open Six-cells. Some guys had moved from their Six-cell to the girls' side because, at this point, who could stop them? Most of the older kids didn't mind the young ones in their Six-cell, but every door was decorated with a hand-drawn sign of a kid that resembled Chuck Hayge with his skivvies around his ankles, a line streaming from the figure, and a giant X drawn through the picture. No one new had entered James and Abe's room because Abe had added an equal sign to the picture and drew a kid strapped naked to a steel frame in the Corral covered in fallen snow.

"Everyone here?" Abe asked.

Everyone looked around as if the absent person would raise a hand to show his or her nonexistence.

"Well, if not, too bad," Abe said. James stood next to Abe. Elise huddled the girls into small groups that crowded close together to keep warm. The guys, with the exception of the youngest who were allowed into the cracks of the girls' huddle, were *too cool* to hug one another in the excessive cold, even if it meant blue cheeks, chattering teeth, and frozen intestines.

"We get it," Abe said.

Everyone looked at one another, confused. James looked at Abe because he *knew* he had missed the point.

"It's cold." Abe's breath hung in the air with a revelatory tint that caught everyone by surprise. "Maybe we don't have to be."

"And the Pope shits in the woods," Geoff said. He ended up in Fornland with the same sarcastic look that straddled his face now. He always said his parents were doctors traveling around the globe to help people. The rumor said they contracted Ebola in Sierra Leone. James found out they used to beat the hell out of each other, probably until their wrists were swollen and eyes were almost dangling out of their heads. When the carnage cleared from each other's bodies they moved onto Geoff. It turned out the only thing that killed Geoff's mom was his father; from what James had read in the papers that Fornland eventually burned to keep warm, nothing had killed Geoff's father. James remembered when Geoff first came to Fornland he had welts on his back and thighs. Geoff hadn't deserved that; no kid did.

"Does the Pope do it in the woods?" Shia, a corral, asked. He was Marcus's best friend. The gaggle of collectives giggled.

"Leave it," Elise said. The gaggle stopped laughing. Shia looked at Abe with wide eyes, hoping that his question would be answered. The closest these kids had ever gotten to woods were the trees in the park, the bears in the zoo, or some book they had found with a decomposed cover rotting on the bookshelf. James smiled.

"It's time to go," James said.

"You think we would have stayed if we had somewhere to go?" Geoff asked. "We would have hightailed it with the rest of the goddamned group."

A sound of agreement went up like birds, birds that hadn't been around since before the snow. The birds had flown south—even those that had never migrated before. Cats ran from their homes and dogs escaped before the first snowflake landed. The zoos closed quickly, but no one knew what to do with the animals inside. The reptiles died early. Some zookeeper who couldn't stand to watch the animals suffer tried to let them all out, hoping they'd survive in the open wild of the empty parks.

No one knew if the zookeeper made it out or if the animals survived but people swore, as their world turned white, that they could hear elephants trumpet and wolves howl. No one ventured into the closed parks; they were too worried about polar bears breaking through the gates and thriving in the ice-covered streets. Rumors of polar bears spotted around the exterior of the parks had lingered in the city's whispers. Geoff called it idiotic, because Geoff would.

The response from the frigid room hit James harder than the menacing air outside.

"Maybe we don't need a place to go," Abe said. "Just a way to get there."

"We'll be the next Amelia Earhart," Geoff said. "A frozen dream come true."

"Don't flatter yourself," Abe said.

"There'll be no one around to remember you disappeared," James said.

The kids laughed. Geoff scoffed, crossed his arms, and leaned back against the cold steel of the bed frame. Everyone looked to Abe for direction or consolation. *It's like the fantasy of firefighting, except instead of saving one baby he will save all of us*, James thought. There was a sense of earnest understanding in his face and his tone. The fear that James knew everyone felt didn't apply to Abe. It never had before.

"We don't have anywhere to go," Abe said, "that's true. But there has to be more out there and I know how to find it."

A glacial quiet settled over the group. No one wanted to speak out against Abe's certainty, his calm demeanor, or his hope. He held a fatherly tone that James heard for the first time and it comforted everyone in the cold.

"Hell has frozen over," Elise said. She looked around the Collective. "Why would anywhere else be different?"

"When was the last time you heard of hot sandy beaches and umbrella drinks?" Abe asked.

The television stations had all gone to ruin, news anchors had run amok without their hair gels and eyebrow trimmers. The radio worked for a while longer. The hard voice of fact pounded through the speakers until the power went out, until the batteries drained, until the hope of connecting to the outside world all but died.

"Two months," Abe said.

James was ready to follow Abe to the ends of the earth in search of heat, in search of anything that would take him out of Fornland and away from the pits of San Diego. James was brought in to the boardinghouse quietly but he wouldn't leave in silence.

"Why not go?" Abe asked. "No reason to stay and I know the way out."

"And why not burn the mother down in the process?" James asked. Abe turned to him and smiled. It hadn't occurred to James before now, before the block around them started to fry. Fornland looked back wide-eyed.

"And why not burn the mother down in the process," Abe said.

# THE SPACE BETWEEN

## JAMES

THE COLLECTIVE EMPTIED, THE MUFFLED SOUND OF SHOES ON soft snow echoing in the hollow room. Charlotte stayed and rubbed her fingers over the bed frame. James stood by the door and waited to be noticed, half-hoping she wouldn't notice him at all and would continue to run her hands over the bed, caught in some reverie of the day she arrived and her last moments before she came to Fornland.

"This was my bed when I first got here," Charlotte said. Her voice was soft in the hard cold. James wasn't sure if she spoke to him or to herself. She looked up at James. "I never liked it, but now, it's like I'm going to miss it or something." She

153

looked back at the mattress, rubbed her hand against the rough fabric, and pushed on the frigid springs. James walked through the maze-like isle of shifted beds and sat close to her—*not too close.*

"Maybe you are," James said. She looked at him, her green eyes a welcome change from the expanse of white and gray that filled the room. Her hair had changed with time. The non-ironic white sat at the tips of her light brown hair, her natural color grown out.

"How can you miss something you never liked?" Charlotte asked.

"I found this," James said. He placed a small stuffed walrus between them. She reached for it and her fingers brushed against his hand. He expected her skin to be cold like the rest of the world, but somehow, she left a touch of warmth on his hand when she pulled the walrus into her arms.

"I thought he would've been burned by now," she said.

"Locked in the Cage in Bernice's office," James said. "No idea why we didn't look in there sooner."

James had looked in the Cage sooner. It was where they kept all the toys, stuffed animals, *personal possessions,* that Fornland couldn't allow the kids to keep after a certain age. It was the first place James checked after the admin left, but, with the exception of Abe, he kept it a secret in case any of the found objects proved useful in the future. The moment he saw the walrus stuffed between an old iPod—that he had stolen from some kid on the trolley but never admitted to—and a unicorn calendar the size of a small dog, James remembered the moment he first saw Charlotte grasping onto the walrus for dear life.

"What's his name?"

"Franklin," Charlotte said. She cradled the walrus between her arms and her chest. "You found this in the Cage?"

"Good name for a walrus," James said. He could feel her eyes on him. A small smile stuck to the corners of her lips. The white tips of her hair tapped at her shoulders like fragile icicles. James half-expected to hear them peal like wind chimes but the haze of silent breaths was all that hung in the air.

"You're kind of weird," Charlotte said.

"Call it a lack of social skills," James said. He stood up to walk out of the room. Weird was more of a compliment than she realized, whether it was meant to be an insult or not. He was ready to leave, take one last look at Fornland from the outside, flip up his middle finger, let it freeze, walk deeper into the snow, and never look back.

"How long have you—" she paused. "I saw you when I first got here. However long ago that was. You've been here for a long time."

"Not much longer now," James said. He made to leave the room but she stopped him.

"Where'd you come from?" Charlotte asked.

"Abandonment," James said. "You?"

"Oceanside," she said. "But it's not that far off."

"Overdose?" James asked. It had become the easiest question to ask Fornland kids, a presumption that didn't hurt. It spoke to an inability to change an inevitable decline of their parents, as opposed to willing abandonment. The kids whose parents had OD'd were looked at as lucky; their parents loved them but were torn away too soon because of an addiction. The ridiculous hierarchy of an orphanage.

"Runaway," she said. "My parents were moving and I didn't want to, so I ran away one day to show them how serious I was. They went looking for me. They never saw the car crash into them." She held Franklin tighter. "At least that's what the cops told me."

"If you can't trust a cop . . . " James said.

"The irony is we were moving to Hawaii. My dad didn't want to ship more than he needed to, so he figured he could use the car as a sort of storage bin. Would have been warm. Could have been good."

"Bright side," James said. She raised her eyebrows. "You figured out what irony means."

Charlotte stood from the bed frame, Franklin clasped in her hands. James stood in the doorway.

# FIRE STARTER

## JAMES

ABE STOOD ANKLE-DEEP IN THE SNOW. FORNLAND KIDS had spent the last two hours with bats, clubs, hammers, and whatever else they could use to break through the walls, tear down the frame, crush the tile, and find whatever they could use to help burn the building down.

"Safety first," Abe yelled. His hands cupped around his mouth.

Everyone screamed, some of the younger kids pounded their chests. The door to Fornland was wide open. When Bernice left and the city started to burn, Abe felt like they became animals in the zoo, escaped from their cages and let loose on the world—let loose on the cages that had held them for decades. They swept out the snow to the entrance; wood lined the floor beneath the tiles. Abe had made the decision not to tear the wood from the entrance earlier. It would have made getting through the boardinghouse that much harder. James took the time to spread around any flammable objects he had found in the Cage. He placed the giant unicorn calendar beneath the stairs and piled a few smaller stuffed animals in a corner. He put a fire extinguisher beneath his sheets in his Six-cell.

"Extinguishers don't explode," Geoff had said.

"Of course they do," Abe answered. "They're filled with pressure. Pressured things explode."

"It's meant to put out fires," Geoff said. "It won't work."

"Only one way to find out," James said.

James stood near Abe outside of Fornland's cracked walls. The hushed fury of broken wood, crumbled papers, and crunching snow reverberated against the entryway.

"Everyone out?" Abe asked.

The group looked around. They had all helped tear open the wood beneath the entryway tiles and spread it through the house. They hoped they had enough wood, enough crap strewn throughout the building to break Fornland down, to burn it and all the memories stuffed inside it.

"Wait," Marcus said. He was almost eight years old. After his dad died, he always had questions, always had bright eyes and a curious smile, even in the cold. Marcus had been in the Corral for over two years. He was one of the few kids, if not the only kid, who James would have considered allowing in his Six-cell. Marcus ran out through the open doors with a book clutched in his hands. James knew the book by the cover, a small boy with blond hair standing on a small planet surrounded by stars. Abe ran through the snow that almost swallowed his knees and took a spot next to James.

"That the last—" Abe said. He pointed to the book. "Why?"

"You shouldn't be afraid of a hat," Marcus said.

"Is that so?" Abe said. "Hey, Hamez! You afraid of hats?"

James looked into the sky, the light stuffed behind the clouds and almost snuffed out. He turned in a circle, crunched snow ruffling beneath his feet. He raised his finger in the air and felt the wind.

"Can't see any reason to be," James said.

"Maybe we'll find desert," Marcus said. The book had been in Fornland longer than Marcus. True to his word, he kept it beneath his bed. No one would've taken it away from him, but when the cold rushed over the building the book was one of the last semblances of paper around. The rest of the books had been pilfered and burned. Abe patted Marcus on the shoulder. Lately Abe had a tone in his voice, an energy to his touch, a pride in his eyes whenever someone did good. It kept everyone wanting to please him. For whatever reason Abe never minded James around and James never knew why. James had been in Fornland for less than a year when Abe was brought into the system with the promise of hot meals and clean sheets. The promise most of them had been misled by.

Abe came into the Corral and was placed on a vomit-stained mattress the admin hadn't taken the time to clean, let alone replace. Abe refused to sleep on it; even at seven Abe was headstrong, defiant, and smart. Most of the corral kids told him to shut up and sleep but he had refused. He said he'd rather sleep on the floor. James stayed quiet until then, when Abe began to place his sheets on the floor and make a bed for the night.

"Abe," James said. His eyes peaked over the bed frame. "Don't do that."

"Don't tell me what to do," Abe said. "And why not?"

"You can share this bed," James said. He wasn't sure why he offered but he did. Bernice told him to show Abe the ropes. James liked that Abe wouldn't take crap from anyone. He stood up for himself against the corral. He stuck to his guns on the mattress. Abe was a person James wished he could be but never would. "Really. Come here."

Abe climbed up onto James's bed.

"You sound serious," Abe said.

Five minutes later Chuck Hayge woke up and screamed, again. He threw his sheets from his body, stood on the bed, and began to preach against the trolls as piss splashed and pooled on the tile, a large group of corral kids joined in again. It wasn't hard to see that Abe would have been soaked in corrals' pee if he hadn't listened to James.

"Thanks," was all Abe had said. It was never as easy to make friends as it had been in that moment.

And now Abe was leading the charge to burn the building. The city block began to reek of petrol.

"I liberated some from the abandoned gas station," Geoff said. James knew that any station in the area had long been looted of its supply. It meant Geoff stole the gasoline from someone else that had either hoarded or abandoned it.

"Hear that, kids?" Abe asked. "Let's get to where we need to be. We'll know it when we see it."

The snow sat quiet beneath everyone's feet. Abe gave the signal to ignite Fornland. Some kids had lighters, some had matches, some kids soaked rags in leftover kerosene, wrapped them around baseball bats, and tried to light them on the pilot light that hadn't worked for two months at least. James flicked his Bic. No spark. He flicked it again. No spark. He wasn't alone in his trouble to get a flame going. Abe seemed to be the only one with a flame in his hands glowing bright on the tip of soaked cloth wrapped around a hammer. Everyone stopped and waited to see what Abe would do. He pulled the flame back, glanced at the warm orange glow, and chucked the hammer inside the icy window. Fragmented ice mixed with the shatter of glass. The hammer flew into Fornland. Quiet fell through the sky with the snow. A flicker of light raised behind the broken window. The flames grew. The acrid smell of burning gas surrounded them.

"Burn like the hell you are!" Elise screamed. Her voice pierced the flames' growing roar. The crowd cheered and the earth seemed to rumble, as much from the flames as from their voices. James's gloves muffled his clapping hands. Ten years of his life burned in front of his eyes. From Charlotte's kiss to now, it felt like he could finally exhale. The Samuel S. Fornland Boarding House was coming to the ground. The crowd had their hands in the air. Hugs and cries, laughter and tears, their feet stomped through the snow, twirling around the mounds, as the heat rose and they all embraced the crack, crash, and fall of their former home.

"It's over," Charlotte said with tears in her eyes.

"Partly," James said. "Something's just beginning."

"Hear that, Hamez?" Abe asked. "We're finally moving on." Abe wrapped his arms around Elise and kissed her fast and hard.

"I will miss our corner though," Elise said as the flames started to roar.

"I'll make you a new one," Abe said.

The sign teetered above the door. THE SAMUEL S. FORNLAND BOARDING HOUSE: WELCOME HOME. A cacophonous boom echoed in the falling sky. The pieces of the house flew everywhere. The fire extinguisher had erupted. Another cry erupted as the cages of their past exploded away.

"I'll be banged sideways," Geoff said.

"I told you," Abe said.

"Pressure can cause explosions," James said.

James could imagine the plaque inside finally leaving the comfort of the entryway, the last remnants of Fornland's heroic deed blowing up and dying in a fire. The words on the sign were hung skewed, scraped above the doorframe, fragile, and melting.

# SNOWFALL AND DIRECTIONS

## JAMES

FORNLAND DISAPPEARED INTO THE ORANGE GLOW AND ACRID haze. Abe stood defiantly in the mixture of ash, snow, and circling smoke, arms at his side, chin raised . . . *Like a dark superhero*, James thought. The kids continued to clap and scream in triumph. Some of the corrals and collectives danced around Abe in a circle. They raised their heads to the sky and howled the way kids always did when excited, when wild and free. James half-expected a polar bear to stretch its paws around them, show its sharp teeth, shout its fierce roar, and shatter the dream they had all dreamt together.

Now that Fornland was gone it was hard to

imagine what the world would be like. Not the entire world, but their world—his world. The smoke began to burn his lungs when he breathed, but he couldn't turn away, compelled to watch the boardinghouse burn down to its final embers. The fire was hot and the smoke was high, which meant trouble would be close. James called over to Abe, his chin still turned up towards Fornland. The sign was a molten puddle at the foot of the entrance. Even if the building continued to stand, remnants of the boardinghouse were gone, except for the kids and what was left of them: their memories and night-mares. *One day, maybe, that will all go too*, James hoped.

"Cut," James said. The howlers stopped. The dancing ceased. The glint in Abe's eyes disappeared, replaced by the reality of the fire in front of them, the proud smile gone from his face.

"Scavs?" Abe asked.

When the windows of the city shattered and the wealthy ran, the scavengers were the assholes that looted, broke, robbed, rotted, and burned the city and anyone in their way. It was early on in the Freeze when La Jolla burned. The televisions still worked then. James watched the fuzzy screen as lampposts were brought down, asphalt torn apart, doors ripped open, and one cherry-red Ferrari wrapped around a fire hydrant. Water thundered into the air; James wondered if the water froze immediately in the sky and came down as snow-flakes or if the torrent was too powerful to freeze in motion. It was the newscaster that called them all scavengers: "Scavengers that took advantage of our troubled times." About a week later, one of the corrals couldn't sleep. Marcus came to get James because Abe was somewhere else, probably with Elise.

"It's Shia," Marcus said with the heavy static of sleep in his voice. Too scared to leave his bed but too timid to cry, James sat at the edge of Shia's bed, his head cocooned beneath his sheets.

"Cold?" James asked. It had become the salute,

like, "How are you?" or "What's up?" Everyone was cold. Everything was cold. It was more about acknowledging the person as opposed to the question as it stood. James put his hand on Shia's shoulder.

It was moments like this that James wished Abe had been there. Abe would know how to comfort and console, with some phrase he heard somewhere in the ether that wouldn't even make sense but somehow made corrals' eyes pop in amazement. James copied what he had seen in old movies: the shoulder touch, the head-cradled hug, the sound of *shh*, and the ability to sit in silence until the inconsolable were ready to be consoled, which was all James could do now—wait in the sounds of Shia's muffled whimpers.

He pulled his head from beneath the sheets. His eyes were red and his cheeks were wet. James rubbed his hand along Shia's forehead, pushing his hair aside like mothers did in movies.

"I thought you were Abe," Shia said. James

wished. He kept quiet and put on a thin smile. Between them was the faint outline of Shia's shallow breaths.

"What's cold?" It was Shia's turn to smile in the glow that all kids have when they are spoken to and known by someone older, when a sense of appreciation washes over.

"I was out this morning," Shia said. "I saw a bunch of guys run into the liquor store around Shelltown. The guy behind the counter pulled out his gun. One-two-three gunshots. There was blood all over the window. They saw me and I ran. Blood ran down the glass. I ran and I ran here."

"You're okay," James said. "They won't come here."

"How do you know?"

"Trust me." Every once in a while James said something that he knew to be right, where he could say "trust me" and know he wasn't full of shit. Fornland was a place of destitution, filled with vagrants. It was a wonder they all hadn't turned into scavengers sooner.

"This isn't the place where scavengers go," James said.

"Scavs?" Shia asked.

A simple evolution of a simple word. *Why should Shia know what a scavenger is when he would never see one, would never need to see one?* James thought. The word could have been the same as any other animal or object he would never know, like rocket ship, beach towel, or French bread.

"Scavs," James said. The name stuck.

The city had run out of riches and warmth. The flames crackled and roared.

"Stay away from fires," the newscaster said in one of the last television broadcasts. It was the reason why James, Abe, and Bernice told Elise to keep clear of the building bashes. "Scavs follow the heat. When flames are present, they think there are leftovers, possibly food, blankets, camping gear, et cetera.

They are even drawn to the idea of a few hours by the fire," the newscaster continued.

Neighborhoods became divided by scavenger packs, the new gangs of the city, all dying and trying to survive on the leftovers of the dead. The house was stuck between two scav cliques. Fornland was never in danger; it would never be ransacked and stripped bare. Scavs knew what Fornland was: filled with a lot of shit and yet completely empty.

"It's one thing to get maybe five people to the docks, but a hundred?" Abe now asked. "I shouldn't have listened to you."

"You just needed a reason to wait," James said. Abe shrugged his shoulders. It would take over two hours to walk to the docks on a good day, when days could have been good and not hunkered down by pounds of snow, piles of corrals and collectives, and neighborhoods flooded with hungry scavs.

"We'll have to go through Shelltown," Abe said.

"I know a guy," James said. He waved Shia over in the quiet. The shuffle of Shia's feet was crisp in the air and quiet on the ground. They would have to move soon and quick. Shia saddled up to James.

"Cold?" Shia said. Abe nodded his head.

"You know where the docks are," James said. Shia nodded. "You know Shelltown." Shia froze; it wasn't from the cold. Abe bent down, eye to eye with Shia.

"Time to lead, little one," Abe said. "You know Shelltown?" Shia nodded again, his shoulders still stiff. "You're our guy." Abe pointed to the kids lingering in Fornland's smoke. Today it became a game of all or nothing.

They had all stayed at Fornland because they had nothing, but James was ready to take it all. They all were. James could tell by how they gave themselves to Abe's plan, to leave Fornland, to ditch San Diego, and to make sure no one could step inside that burnt-out fleapit again. It had come down to the familiar versus the unfamiliar. James had found comfort in the uncomfortable and was willing to let life push him around because that's what life did. Until life pushed too far and James pushed back.

The group meandered in the snow and waited for direction. The once vacant thoughts of the future began to flood with possibility, but not all possibilities were good. The anxiety palpitated in the air to the rhythm of the burning building.

"Time to go," James said.

"How, exactly?" Geoff asked. A group of six-cells nodded and mumbled.

Abe stood behind Shia with his hands on Shia's shoulders, an act of encouragement James wouldn't have thought of. *The kid's got to accept his destiny*, James thought. Surviving abandonment wasn't enough. James wished there were a sign, a giant goddamned sign that said, *Welcome to Destiny*, so he could knock it down, kick a hole through it, and lay it at the center of the fire with the forgotten plaque.

"I'm not putting my life in the hands of a corral," Geoff said.

"No," Abe said.

"Our hands too," James said. "Our lives too."

Geoff scoffed. His six-cells mumbled around him.

"Do you know the way?" Abe asked. "If you know it, take us. If you have a better idea let's follow it. If not—"

"Time's up," James said. He looked at Shia. "Your turn."

Shia stood a bit straighter beneath Abe's hands. Abe gripped Shia's shoulders a bit tighter.

"We need to go that way," Shia said, and began to lead the pack. The whisper of flames hissed louder than their labored footsteps as the building crumbled away behind them.

# ON THE BACKS
# OF SCAVENGERS

## JAMES

James didn't know why the area had been named Shelltown, but the neighborhood was never more true to its name. The streets were barricaded in parts, homes were burned or torn down, and cars were overturned. A war had been and was still fought on the streets, but it was anybody's guess as to which streets would be crowded with gunshots, baseball bats, and stolen knives. It was a wonder any part of the street was still visible. Even under the mounds of snow and frozen pathways, Shelltown looked like a shell more now than ever, shattered and scattered.

"They're usually around there," Shia pointed

to the far corner. *How can they sneak this many people around an entire neighborhood?* James wondered. He was about to find out. It would have been easier to break through the zoo and take on the wild animals; at least James would have known what to expect. Wild animals were predictable, in part, but scavs were senseless. *I'd rather take my chances with the polar bears.*

"We can avoid the corner completely if we . . . " Shia's words trailed into murmurs. His eyes went vacant. James and Abe looked around, worried that they had been discovered. It wasn't what could happen that turned Shia immobile, but what had happened.

"The liquor store?" James asked.

Shia nodded. Tears began to fill his eyes.

"This is why you can't trust a corral," Geoff said. James gave Geoff the universal stare to shut the hell up. Whether Geoff noticed it or not, he shut the hell up.

"Blink it away, little one," Abe said. "It's your show."

Shia wiped at his unshed tears, sniffed his nose, and nodded. James didn't expect the walk to be this quiet. He expected more of the post-apocalyptic detriment from movies; he expected a lack of water, sprawling deserts, burnt-out cars, and shelled-out cities. The plush white blanket that covered the city, the world even, didn't look like the barren landscape promised in the aftermath of wars, the world taken by man's egotistical superiority in the belief that they could manipulate the earth without consequence.

James spit. Movies didn't prepare him for this world. Nothing could have.

"Same plan," Abe told James. "I'll take the front with Shia. You take the back; make sure no one is left behind. Geoff, you take the middle." James watched Geoff set off. The guy needed to keep his mouth shut, Captain Obvious incarnate, able to name all the problems, crap on solutions, but never able to come up with a solution of his own. It's a wonder he came with the group in the first place; he could have set off on his own months ago with the rest of the deserters and adventurers.

"I know," Abe said. "Giving him something to do shuts him up." *That's what good friends do,* James thought, *know what the other was thinking most often.* The thought had been easy: *who didn't want Geoff to shut up?*

Shia led the group through an alley two-and-a-half streets up from the scavs' corner, one long stretch of narrow street that would take them past the liquor store where Shia had watched the blood splatter against the window. Fences lined the entire alleyway, which meant if there were scavs squatting somewhere around the street, the group would be dead meat and the scavengers would come calling.

Shia and Abe went first. James listened for the sound of crunched ice beneath their feet. James's heavy breath filled his ears; the sound of ice didn't. The first wave of six had made it across the street, down the alley, and towards the liquor store. The second wave of six followed. Each group had three corrals or collectives with three six-cells, hands held and eyes wide. They all knew how to forage, how to run, and how to hide, but they didn't know how to do it in such a large group.

There was a manner of togetherness between them, but James knew that at the first sign of trouble their hands would come apart. They would throw one another to the ground and everyone would run their separate ways. James wanted to avoid that at all costs. This was the plan they had. There was no backup plan. The third and the fourth groups ran down the alley, then the fifth and the sixth. Charlotte went on the ninth wave. James watched her white tips blend into the fallen snow and wished he were on the opposite side of the alley where he could watch her eyes come closer to him. The gray sky sunk over them, almost able to touch. Charlotte looked back at him, a quiet gesture.

Two groups remained, James at the end with his hand wrapped tight around Marcus's. The alley seemed longer than before. The majority of the group on the other side was sheltered by the liquor store of Shia's nightmares, but it was the one place that the scavs had looted enough to not bother again, whether the bloodstained window remained or not.

When the scavs were seen rioting on television, there was a group of kids who wanted to join them, who felt they had earned the right to jump into the massive crowd of broken people and split open the city. Some did go; James almost wished that Geoff had gone.

Elise came to James one day holding Marcus's elbow, dragging him along. She looked pissed; he looked uncomfortable.

"I found him and a few others going to join the scavs by the Gaslamp District," she said. She let go of Marcus's arm. He watched the ground. He hadn't fit into his Spiderman shoes in a long time, but the look was the same. "We can't help them if they don't want it, but Christ, James, they're just kids." Her voice was low.

"We all are," James said. "I'll take care of it." Elise walked away. Her footsteps echoed against the concrete walls.

"You want to be tough, kid?"

"I am tough," Marcus whimpered.

"I remember," James said. "Crier."

Marcus ran at James and tried to tackle him to the ground. He screamed and grunted. James didn't move.

"I want to show you something. You want to be a scav?"

James dragged Marcus out of Fornland and through the snow. Marcus wasn't able to keep up with James's furious walk. James held Marcus by the elbow and squeezed hard.

"That hurts," Marcus said.

"You're a tough guy. Deal with it." When they got to a metal gate a few blocks away from

Fornland, James ducked down behind a car. Frost washed over the blue color. He pulled Marcus with him. "You know what it takes to be a scav?" he whispered. Marcus shook his head. James pointed to the fence. Heads, torn and covered in icy blood topped the metal spikes. Each face was frozen in horror forever or until the snow thawed.

"They tear off people's heads and use their skin as coats to keep warm," James said. "Whatever it takes . . . they're not human." Marcus nodded. "Understand?" Marcus nodded again.

Now, with Fornland burned to the ground behind them, they had to march through a whole neighborhood of scavengers as if the cold hadn't been enough.

James heard a crunch, the quiet crunch of ice breaking. None of them could have caused it. The world started to smell of decay and the crunch became louder and fuller. Louder. Fuller. It almost screamed, "Here we are! We've got you!" Marcus squeezed James's hand. James tried to shield

Marcus from the unspoken fear in his eyes. He needed to ask: "Did you hear it?" Marcus didn't understand. James tapped Tic-Tac, another six-cell. Tic-Tac turned, ready to say, "What?" James stopped him by wrapping his free hand over Tic-Tac's mouth. Tic-Tac wanted to back away but didn't. His ears perked in the quiet gray and James knew that Tic-Tac understood.

Tic-Tac tapped the remainder of the group, both young and old, and put his finger to his lips. The crunch of ice had subsided but James didn't trust it. It was a practice they had all become familiar with over the months, even if not in as large of a group. They learned how to whisper their needs in the silent frozen air, surrounded by the noisy stench of death. The scavs had gotten smart in the past weeks, at least in this area; it wasn't hard to figure out that screaming and running towards their victims made their prey run away, but if the scavs snuck up and surprised their victims they wouldn't have to work as hard.

One crunch, soft, small, slow. A second, slower. James counted the time between the crunches, like thunder after lightning, like heartbeats in his throat. He watched the alley and listened for a heavy breath, a dangled chain, a whispered sound. Were they in the alley? Were scavs behind them? Were they down the street? There was a push against the gate they stood next to, a tender thud against the frozen wood.

James found them next to him, next to the last two groups. They had to run. If they fled down the alley they would lead the scavs to the rest of the group. There had to be another way, another direction—a plan B.

Plan A was about to be torn apart by beasts of desperation. They never had a plan B. Scavs strived to live day to day. They burned what they could, wore what they could, ate what they could. James would be goddamned if he would be skinned half-alive so his head could be used as a cap to keep these undead bastards alive for one more day. Scavs wore their victims' skin like rubber suits to keep themselves warm as their clothes and sanity deteriorated with time.

James squeezed Marcus's hand tighter. Marcus's big brown eyes looked up, and were filled with fear. He understood. James nodded to Tic-Tac, the silent agreement to push, run, live. He now knew too. James signaled Abe. Abe took Shia by the hand and disappeared into the liquor store. They had to run all the way to the goddamned port without the rest of Fornland. They'd meet up later if they could. It's the only choice they had. It was James's choice to be a hero, to hold the baby and jump through the flames.

"Scatter!" James said. The last two groups emptied from their hiding and sprawled into the street. A dozen scavs hopped over the fence and landed where James had been. The group sped down the alley. Screams and snarls followed them. The scavs slapped their crowbars against the fences, scratching their chains on the ice. A collected thunder ran behind James.

"Keep going," James said. They all knew not to run into the liquor store. They were lucky the last two groups were smaller, but the corrals and collectives had trouble keeping up. Their legs were smaller, their lungs were smaller, their arms were smaller, but they had will.

James could hear the heavy breath and snarls of the scavs, but he refused to look back. Marcus's hand was slick with sweat. Marcus held on tight. James's breath was short. Marcus started to slow.

"Rocket," James screamed. Marcus continued slowing. James's body pumped with fear and adrenaline, caught in his eyes and pulsing in his veins.

"You've got to try," James said. *Fucking scavs.* A few wore coats, frayed and patched all around. A few wore layers of clothes, flannel button-downs wrapped on top of torn t-shirts too big for their hollowed bodies, any extra fabric they found filled the space where air could creep in. Some, the smallest of them, didn't even have complete shoes. The material was worn or torn, and parts of socks and toes were open and out to a world that would soon swallow their appendages whole. The scavs' faces were twisted with anger, not anger built from hatred, but anger that stemmed from fear. No one knew how long they would last, between the cold freezing them to their bones and the scavs scavenging to survive. Those who might have predicted the predicament were cozied up somewhere in a bunker beneath the dirt where they could hold their hands to heaters, eat canned soup, and sleep beneath unfrozen blankets.

The tormented cries of the scavs came closer. James had lost sight of the rest of the group. They must have found safety and circled back to the liquor store. He could feel his heart beat in his throat and was ready to choke on it. Marcus's grip loosened.

"The book!" Marcus said. He pulled at James.

For a moment, hot sweat dripped down James's cheeks. He could have sworn it turned to ice before it hit the ground.

"We can't leave it," Marcus said.

The distance between them and the book grew. The distance between them and the scavs shrank.

"We have to keep going," James said. He pulled on Marcus's hand. The strain was tangible. Marcus tried to plant his feet. James began to drag Marcus along the ice. "Keep moving!" James would drag Marcus all the way to the port if he had to, if he could. He would carry the child out of the flames and be the hero, the hero he needed to be, for himself, for Marcus, for Fornland.

Marcus's hand slipped. All that was left between James's fingers was stale air. James tried to stop, plant his feet, grab Marcus. James slipped instead. The ice brought him to the ground. A scrape of cold scratched his cheeks. A piercing ring hit his ears. The air escaped from his lungs.

Marcus ran. The book glowed against the ice.

James tried to stand. The ground had sucker-punched him. It twinged. *Run. Get Marcus. Scream. Get help. Help Marcus. Get up and help him.* The words didn't come. The air didn't come. The sound didn't come. *Did Marcus not notice the scavs? Leave the book and go!* But James stayed curled up on the ice, watching. Marcus made his way to the book. The scavs made their way to Marcus. Marcus's arms flew, his legs kicked, a trail of snow floated behind him. The gnarled faces of the scavs grew. The putrid smell of decay filled the street. The scavs descended. Their screams punctured the silence. The book was in Marcus's hands. James saw it. Marcus had made the grab. He had turned. The scavs jumped. They screamed—cried. Beat one another. A cry. A crunch. The terrible ring filled James's ears.

In the distance James saw a slight movement of white on white, a four-legged figure large and lumbering. The grunts and scrapes of the scavs caught its attention. The polar bear looked over. Its black eyes peered at the chaos. It stepped and sniffed the air. James wanted to look into its dark eyes, ask it for help, see its sharp teeth charge in James's direction. The bear slowly turned away, frightened by the commotion. James took a breath. Then there was silence. He couldn't see Marcus anymore.

# WHAT WAS LEFT

## JAMES

JAMES PUSHED OPEN THE DOOR TO THE LIQUOR STORE. The blood-splattered window filled the expanse of the store's façade like a spider web as Shia had described it. The tiny bell pealed a high-pitched ding through the broken, empty shelves when James opened the door. The ring was a sound James wanted to run from. It was the same ring in his ears when Marcus disappeared in the swarm.

James had crawled out of sight and hid until the cries were gone, until the scrape of chains and knives were gone, until, he had hoped, he would walk into the open, grab Marcus, and make it to the liquor store. He had known what would be left of Marcus once the scavs left. More importantly, he knew what wouldn't be left.

The scavs had dispersed, crawling back into the pits from which they came. The scavs were satisfied with their take, at least for the moment, and James left his cold crawl space. He stepped into the street and saw a mass of dark red snow, what would have been a puddle of blood for a second, seeped into the white and stained the street. Marcus was gone. James had known he would be, but James had survived on hope for so long that sometimes it blinded him to what he already knew. Next to the crimson snow was the book, spattered with spit and blood. James picked it up, wiped it with his sleeve and left to meet the others.

The book was a reminder of the baby he couldn't save in the flames he couldn't jump through. Every step he took filled him with more grief. *Abe could have saved Marcus. Abe would have saved Marcus. I'm nothing like Abe and never will be.*

James ignored the window. The shelves were

barren and broken. The stench of cold musk filled the store; no corrals, no collectives, no six-cells, no Charlotte, no Abe. James wandered through the decrepit aisles, over the torn-up shelves, and into the storage room. There was a heavy struggle to his steps; he was too tired to lift his feet. He was caught between wanting to break down the walls of the liquor store and break himself down. *I should have saved him.* Now he couldn't even save himself. There were no potato chips, no Twinkies, no root beer, no booze, and no people. The frozen cardboard of collapsed boxes was all that was left.

James sat with his back to the wall. He put his head to his knees and was ready to give into a sleep he knew he needed but didn't want. *If Marcus's face is already everywhere, then where will it be when I close my eyes?* James thought. The dark gray of a cold sunset began to creep into the room. James had spent so long wanting to be alone in the crowded halls of Fornland, but in the quiet liquor store, with the unbearable ringing in his head, all he wanted was to be back in the halls of the boardinghouse watching Terren search his pillow for lice because Abe had told him that the thread count meant how many lice the factory had found in the fabric before it was sold.

"Hamez," Abe whispered. James couldn't see him. He stood up. "Where's Marcus?" A sliver of light shined through the back door where Abe's voice trailed. James felt a dizzy rush, his stomach twisted, and he tasted the acid rising in his throat. He could give plenty of excuses as to how they had gotten separated. The kids didn't need to know the truth about Marcus. He became a scav, set to wander through the tundra with the unleashed beasts of nature until the end of time. The more James thought about Marcus, the more he wanted to lie—to keep Marcus alive, to help Marcus survive, to help keep himself a hero instead of a definite failure. James's chest ached, heaved, and he vomited over the cardboard floor. It poured from his mouth and burned his nose. He wiped whatever remnants were left from his face. He pulled a string of excess vomit from his lips.

The door opened wider and the group began to pour in. Charlotte moved towards James.

"We heard the bell," she said. "We thought you might have been a scav."

The acrid scent of vomit filled the room.

"Let's go," Abe said, as if he understood. *He probably did*, James thought. No one moved. Not yet.

"Where's Marcus?" Shia asked. He pointed to the book clutched in James's hand. The faint bloodstains on the cover hid in the darkness.

# HOLD ON THE FUTURE

## JAMES

THE LIQUOR STORE WAS FILLED WITH FORNLAND ESCAPING the painful cold. They were safe near the over-looted shelves. Abe tried to thaw some of the cardboard pieces and start a fire using his almost emptied lighter. The flame flickered dimly but worked its way onto the soggy material.

"You're not worried that'll bring scavs?" Charlotte asked.

"We're covered," Abe said, pointing to the blood-smeared window.

James looked away from the blood. He couldn't help but see the pool left by Marcus's absent body smeared in the snow.

"Stop it," Elise hushed. "Don't scare them." She nodded to the corrals and the collectives. "They've been through enough today." *We all have*, James thought.

"Cold?" Shia asked. He sat down next to James. "What happened?" His voice was soft. James could feel the heat rushing to his cheeks, pulsing in his eyes. There was time for truth. They all wanted to know, but did they need to? They needed to hear whatever it would take for them to survive.

The flames licked at the cardboard, giving a hazy light to the room.

"You remember your first day in Fornland?" James asked. Shia shook his head. "Lots of people don't. There were rumors once that everyone was born alone, all orphans. It made me think about why some people aren't, or what it takes—I don't know."

"I remember Marcus's first day."

James opened *The Little Prince* and started to read. The voice didn't sound like his. The words sounded distant and perverted. The longer James read, the warmer the room became. The flames flickered and shadows blossomed on the walls.

The words from the book echoed through the hollow room. James read the Little Prince's words as if they were his own, as if the Little Prince's words, told through James, could make them all feel better. James let the words from the end of the book overtake the room and offer a better understanding of Marcus's death than James could have provided. James had once told stories about storms and waves, each element shaping and creating the kids of Fornland, but at that moment it didn't seem right. Marcus hadn't cried out when the scavs overtook him. In James's mind, Marcus had fallen gently. Similar words formed in the message of the book. James hesitated. "Marcus had fallen quietly," James told everyone. "Because of the . . . " He closed the book with his voice caught in his throat, cleared the sadness away, and said, "Snow."

He tried to wipe away flecks of blood and held the book tight in his arms.

*We don't have to wait here. We don't have to be fearful and cold. We don't have to cry.*

Muffled whimpers mixed with the uncomfortable shifting of people's bodies. No one knew what to do so they basked in the silence.

The fire started to build, but James knew it wouldn't last long. The cardboard was soggy after it thawed. James could see the half-sunken faces of Fornland in the dim light. Abe's eyes looked from James to the book. Abe didn't have to say anything. James didn't have to speak, he knew.

*We need something to burn if we're going to stay here and keep the fire going,* said the look on Abe's face.

*If you burn the book, I'll burn you with it,* was James's silent reply. The silence passed in an uncomfortable smoke.

# WHERE THE LOST GO

## JAMES

J AMES STOOD IN A SHARED WHISPER OF TIRED CHILDREN. HE pretended to watch the city pass them by. The port was void of people, and cars were left to rot beneath the fallen snow. The group followed Abe through the remainder of the wasteland. The rest of the journey had been quiet, at least for James. They wandered around the sunken streets, through the mounds of snow, and made it to the port; Charlotte held his hand the entire way. He hadn't felt that warm in months, but now it was as if his body could melt the snow beneath his feet. It was filled with an angry heat, a shamed heat, an inability to move forward if he hadn't been helped.

The moon shined bright in the night sky. The sun had stopped heating the earth and the earth's core seemed to have given up, but when the clouds split, the moon glowed bright over the city. The lone cruise ship stood tall along the frozen shore. The cruise liner was a sight, tall, proud, and empty. They wandered along the frozen water until they came to the ship's hull. The ramp up to the inner corridor was in place. Abe led the way and James was near the back. *How could no one have tried to take the ship, especially if the ramp was still set?* The rich, the desperate, the pirates, the thieves, anyone really—the ship was ready to be boarded and sailed, but instead it stood empty.

The rumble of the ramp quieted as they entered the lobby. The carpet had kept some of its color; swirls of blue, red, and green guided them deeper into the ship. The group came to a balcony, circled around the lobby, and stopped. Their mouths were wide and the foyer was bright. A chandelier lit the room, the lights dripping from the golden wire like raindrops. James thought he would never see a sky filled with melted snow again. Here the glass raindrops stood suspended in the air like a static waterfall dripping down to a tiled floor. It was the first chandelier James had ever seen in person and he never wanted to stop looking at it.

"Spread out," Abe said. "Let's get a good look at the boat and scramble from this hole."

Light danced around the room like a ribbon of color that almost layered the lobby. Charlotte squeezed James's hand. The static waterfall returned to its light fixture form. Shuffling feet echoed down the hallways, through open doors, even to the tile below.

"Hamez," Abe said. "To the engine room!" Abe lifted his leg and pointed his finger in the air. It was an explorer's pose. They had created it when they were in the Corral. The corrals would push all the beds together and wrestle on the mattresses; the aim was to push every other kid off of the bed frames, and once you had disposed of the others, plant your leg at the headboard, lift your finger into the air, and claim victory. The game faded out of their lives after a while, but the pose continued, ventured beyond the victorious, and into their daily movements from the Corral to breakfast, from class to the yard, or just when they felt like they had a good idea. This was Abe's attempt to bring James back to reality—a vacant reality that they were trying to fill by escaping the one they had burned down and left smoldering and leaking in the snow.

"Let's," James said. Charlotte held tight to James's hand.

"I'll go check where the captain sits," Charlotte said.

"The bridge," Abe said.

"Why not," she said. She loosened her fingers around James's hand but he wasn't ready to let go. He wasn't ready to let her hand slip from his like he had Marcus's. She patted his hand. Her eyes implored him, assured him. They shone green, the green he wanted to see spread throughout the blue and white world they were stuck in.

"Careful yourself," she said. She winked.

"I'll come with," James said. "You know where it is?"

"Eventually," Abe said. He grabbed Elise's hand and the four of them headed for the bridge.

They stood on the bridge and looked over the ice field that San Diego had become and that the shoreline was becoming. Smoke continued to rise in the distance, a reminder of the fires that weren't and the stolen world that was. It had all been taken away: their youths, their homes, their lives, and it smoldered before them as a reminder they were the ones who almost got out. James wondered if any of the wisps were from Fornland, if the smoke was the last remnant of the boardinghouse.

They had been outside of Fornland for less than twelve hours but somehow it started to feel like a distant memory that had taken place in a sleep now long gone. The world remained as they all knew it, but in the depths of James's mind sat the world as he dreamed it could have been, where the water was a warm blue and the trees were smothered in sap and not layers of ice. The closer they had gotten to the ship, the more the memories merged in that space between dreams. It was hard to tell what was real anymore when reality was too surreal to live in.

"I'll see if the computers work," Charlotte said.

"Let's check if there's a map of the engine room," Abe said.

"Someone has to make sure the rest of them aren't tearing this place apart," Elise said.

The window began to fog from the heat of their combined hard breaths. James ran his finger through the steamed glass and drew a happy face. He could feel the ice form outside, almost as if it crept through the barrier. That was the world now, the constant creeping of the cold through any and every space available.